I0670362

KILLA CREW

WHAT'S YOURS IS MINE

ARYANNA

LOCKDOWN PUBLICATIONS AND CA$H PRESENTS

First Edition 2024

Printed in the United States of America

Lock Down Publications

P.O. Box 944

Stockbridge, GA 30281

www.lockdownpublications.com

Like our page on Facebook: Lock Down Publications

www.facebook.com/lockdownpublications.ldp

This book is dedicated to all the jackboys and jackgirls who are willing to get their hands dirty for a piece of the American dream.

ACKNOWLEDGMENTS

All glory is given to God first and foremost because without Him, I am nothing. I have to thank my fans for still pushing me and motivating me to let the pen bleed on these pages. I have to thank my family, including my in-laws, because you matter more than you know. To my beautiful Shatavia, I love you like hot wings! Lol! You better stay Team Edward for life! Vampire shit! Special shout out to cuz (like a Lebron James chase down)! You know that I fuck wit you, my dude! Shout out to Tasha Lee because I miss you like every fucking day! I gotta thank my LDP FAM for the love and support. I feed off of your energy too. Shout out to my African connection, Malik "21" Kawa. I'm on the way back home, bruh. Let me take a minute and show some love to Deandrea "Naomi"!!! You better know that this shit can still go REALLY FUCKING GOOD OR REALLY FUCKING BAD! lol! Get at me b4 I get mad! BTW, Alexis, stop acting light skin! It's all love though. Heyyyyy, Nessa! Lol! Shout out to my niggas behind the g-wall counting them days. Stay dialed in to that real nigga radio! To anybody that I forgot, I apologize, and I still love you. To all my kids, I love you every day whether we talk or not. Shout out to FAT BABY for keeping it day 1 official!!!! Where would I be without you??? I'll be right back wit another banger next month!

STAY CONNECTED WITH US!

Text **LOCKDOWN** to 22828 to stay up-to-date with new releases, sneak peaks, contests and more...

Like our page on Facebook:
Lock Down Publications

Join Lock Down Publications/The New Era Reading Group

Visit our website:
www.lockdownpublications.com

Follow us on Instagram:
Lock Down Publications

Email Us: We want to hear from you!

1

JAKWAN

Orlando, Florida

"What's the count?"

"I'm looking at five different heat signatures in the house, two downstairs and three upstairs," Jayson replied.

"So, we're outnumbered again," Blaze said.

When I turned around and looked in the back of the van we were sitting in, locking eyes with Blaze, him and Fabian started chuckling. They believed, like I did, that our team of four could take on, and take out, anyone that we were up against, and so far, no one had proven us wrong yet. Some people might call that luck, or even say that we were just having a good run, but the reality was that neither of those things were true. We were having our way out here in these streets because, at the end of the day, we didn't give a fuck about nobody except each other, and so each man was his brother's keeper. We were organized, almost obsessively meticulous, and we tried to always plan for the unexpected.

When shit went bad though, as it did from time to time, we rose to the challenge accordingly and killed without mercy or conscience. When it came to survival, it was never a choice between us and them because it was *always* us and never them.

"Fabian, give me the rundown again," I requested, turning back to look through the windshield at the mini mansion in the distance.

"The house is owned by Hugh and Florence Myers, and they share it with their three kids, ages eight, nine, and eleven. Florence is a stay-at-home mom, and Hugh works for a hedge fund company. All of that only exists on paper though because neither Hugh nor Florence existed eight years ago. Based on the photographs, I'd say that the kids are theirs, but everything else is a lie built by the people that they work for. Twice a week, they get scheduled visitors, one to drop of the product and the other to pick up the money. The money pickup isn't scheduled until tomorrow, and the product should be in there since we eliminated the main person they supply to last week. It's hard to find someone on short notice to move almost fifty keys of fentanyl, especially if they haven't done it before."

"What's the estimated amount that they're holding?" I asked.

"Based on the fact that Mr. and Mrs. Myers wash about $300K a week and funnel it through shell corporations offshore, along with their extensive bitcoin portfolio, I'd say it's a few million at least," Fabian replied.

"Have you already hit all of their financial holdings?" Blaze asked.

The sound of Fabian's fingers flying across his laptop

echoed throughout the van as we all waited for confirmation.

"Their total nest egg was just shy of $52 million... and it's ours now," Fabian stated proudly.

"Mask up. Jayson, you and I will take the front door, and Blaze, you cover the back until we let you in. Everyone clear on their position?" I asked.

Once they all replied affirmatively, we waited on Fabian to work some more of his magic. We weren't an effective team simply because we were ruthless to our core. It was because everybody knew that they had a position to play in order for us to be successful. Fabian's computer skills were second to no MIT graduate, even though he'd acquired his knowledge from a former mentor who'd made hacking an art form. Blaze was the quickest with a gun, almost like someone out of an old black and white Western movie, but pistols weren't the only things that he played with. He was our demolition's expert, and as of yet, there hadn't been anywhere that we couldn't get inside of. With Blaze, there was no such thing as something being impenetrable. Jayson was the devil who fixated on the details, so when we chose a target, he became the invisible man in order to walk around in that target's mind to pick it apart for weaknesses. I considered myself to be the alpha amongst alphas because I was the nigga that they'd follow into hell blindly, and that type of loyalty had been forged by many different fires. Our history together stretched the decade of our twenties, and now, we were big stepping into our dirty thirties with bigger and better plans for our future, beginning with this nice summer night in 2027.

"The security system is now in my control, so any calls for help come to me and only me. Go get it," Fabian said.

I made sure that the thin rubber mask was securely and evenly pulled over my face, successfully turning my God given chocolate skin into that of a pale white man. The fact that despite the dirt we'd done, the world thought we were white instead of Black, made us all laugh inside. It was silent payback for years of oppression. My gloves were pulled on to conceal my hands, and when I looked over at the passenger seat, I saw that Jayson was just as ready in disguise as I was. With our matching blue suits, we looked like Bible salesmen just making our rounds in the sleepy suburban neighborhood, masking our intent of nefariousness.

"Give us a full thirty second count after we breach before you follow," I said, directing my words toward Blaze.

After checking to make sure my Smith & Wesson .357 snub nose revolver was loaded, I tucked it into my suit pocket and calmly got out of the van. Dusk had just surrendered the fight to nighttime and its nocturnal creatures, which allowed us to move with the stealth of shadows. When we arrived on the front porch, I rang the doorbell, and we waited with the patience of a leopard lurking in the high grasses of the African safari.

"Hi, can I help you?" Hugh asked, pulling the front door open.

"Yes, I believe that you can," I replied.

Jayson didn't say shit. He simply raised his .40 cal Desert Eagle and placed it right under Hugh's left eye socket.

"Step backwards slowly," I instructed.

When he complied, Jayson walked into the house with his gun still on Hugh's face, and I followed.

"Where's Florence?" I asked.

"She-she's not here. I'm alone," he lied.

"Listen, you can bullshit if you want to, but it doesn't end well for you or anyone else in this house," I warned.

Hugh kept his mouth closed, and I could immediately read the defiant look in his eyes. I really didn't have the time or patience for his bullshitting though.

"Do it," I commanded.

A split-second later, Jayson pulled the trigger, causing half of Hugh's head to vanish like it had never been there, as his body flew backwards and landed awkwardly. I pulled my own gun out, and as expected, Florence came running from somewhere in the back of the house to find out what was going on.

"If you scream, your kids die too," I warned.

Her feet stopped moving less than a foot away from her husband's body, but her eyes didn't go to his ruined face. They remained locked on me.

"What do you want?" she asked dispassionately.

It was clear for me to see in her eyes that this wasn't her first dead body or murder, nor were the risks of the game that she was playing something to be unexpected. She dressed and accessorized well enough to fit in with the white society she'd entrenched herself in, but Florence wasn't a typical white girl. Her English was flawless, but the faintest hint of a Russian tongue could be heard.

"We want the money and the product, and yes, we know that your kids are upstairs," I replied.

"Then you should also know that, by now, they're locked in the panic room, along with the money and product, and the security alarm has already been triggered. You've got less than two minutes before you end up as dead as my late husband."

The smirk on her face matched the look of secret victory in her eyes, but neither bothered me because I'd seen both before until my target realized that my way was the only way.

"Go let Blaze in," I said, glancing briefly at Jayson.

While he moved out of sight toward the back of the house, I kept my gun trained on Florence and waited patiently.

"I don't know who you are, but I can assure you that I'm not bluffing about help coming, and it ain't the police. You're fucking with an enterprise run by the Cubans, Dominicans, and Haitians, which means that you just picked a fight with a three headed monster," she said.

"They could have more heads than a hydra, and it *still* wouldn't mean a damn thing right now in this moment. The only thing that matters right now is if you're willing to sacrifice the lives of your children to protect some drug money."

"I knew the risks when I signed up for the rewards," she replied nonchalantly.

Her words sounded good, even rehearsed for moments such as these, and they were designed to make any common jackboy question his mission. Me and my niggas were far from average though. I aimed my pistol at her right knee first, and then, I pulled the trigger with no remorse or feeling of hesitation. The .357 jumped in my hand, but I'd anticipated this, so my body absorbed the kickback. Her body didn't fair so well, as her knee exploded, and she collapsed next to her husband. "Death is assured to all of us, but there are things worse than death. I promise," I said, standing over top of her with my gun aimed at her good knee. I knew that my 6'4", two hundred eighty pounds cast a shadow big enough to put the fear of creation's end into anyone, but I could still see the defiance in her cobalt blue eyes. A few moments later, Jayson was back by my side, towering over Florence with his 6'2", two hundred fifty pound frame, and Blaze boxed her in with his 6'2", two hundred forty pound presence standing on the opposite side of her. If Fabian had been with us to add his 6'3", two hundred sixty pounds of pressure to the mix, then Florence would've gotten a good look at the guardians to hell in all of our glory. The shadow of fear that finally appeared on her face told me that it was unnecessary anyway.

"I-I can't open the panic room, only one of the men coming to kill you can," she murmured, still holding the remains of her blood gushing kneecap.

"Let us worry about getting inside, and you just tell us where the panic room is," I replied.

"Up-upstairs, hidden in my bedroom closet."

I nodded toward both of my partners, who headed for the stairs, and then I grabbed a fistful of Florence's chestnut brown hair.

"Come with me," I demanded, dragging her 5'2", one hundred ten pounds like she was a bag of laundry.

By the time we got upstairs, Blaze had his headset on, talking to Fabian, and he was standing in front of the palm scanner. Jayson stood off to the left with his gun pointed at the still closed door.

"I'm doing it now," Blaze said, placing his palm on the scanner.

A few seconds later, the door hissed open.

"H-how did you do that?" Florence asked.

I put my gun to her head as I leaned down over her.

"It's magic," I replied, pulling the trigger and blowing her brains out the side of her skull.

I let her lifeless body drop and turned my attention to the sounds of the crying children. I motioned for them to come out of the panic room into the bedroom, and the two boys and girl complied reluctantly while holding hands. I could tell that one of the boys was the oldest just based on his size, so I decided to address him as the new leader of his family.

"I want you to listen to what I say, and I promise not to hurt you. Do you understand?" I asked.

He nodded, but the look in his eyes was a guarded, distrustful one.

"Clean it out," I said, gesturing toward Blaze and Jayson while nodding toward the panic room.

While they got down to work, I contemplated what I wanted to do with the three newly orphaned children standing before me. To an ordinary person, these were innocent lives that needed to be protected, but my eyes saw witnesses and liabilities. The only thing that pricked my conscience was the intimate understanding I had of what it was like to be orphaned as a byproduct of violence. I knew that pain, but I also knew what motivation that pain could be because it was my baptism by fire. I took the ten minutes that it took Jayson and Blaze to gather and remove what we'd came for giving serious thought to what it meant to have history repeat itself, and I finally arrived at a decision.

"We got everything, and Blaze is working on the house," Jayson said, stopping beside me.

I nodded, and he waited to see what my next move was.

"Get your brother and sister and follow me," I instructed, looking at the oldest of the three children.

Once the little boy nodded, I led the way back downstairs and outside into the humid night air, not stopping until we were standing across the street from their house. I turned my attention back to the kids then.

"You all stay right here until someone comes to help you. If you go back into your house, you will die. Understand?" I asked.

No one spoke, but the older boy nodded in understanding. Feeling like I'd done my good deed for the day, I left them there and climbed into the van with Jayson following my lead.

"Blaze, do it," I said, starting the van and pulling away fast.

A few seconds later, all anyone heard was a deafening explosion that could be felt reverberating through the ground. In the rearview mirror, the flames leaping toward the sky looked like a beautiful sunrise at the beginning of a promising day.

2

KYNDRA

Washington D.C.

"So, are we getting out of here or what?"

"You're very direct, and I must admit that I like that in a man. I like the type who knows how and when to take charge, a true dominant force the way that God intended you to be," I replied, gazing into his eyes with a look of practiced enchantment.

"I'm very direct, and I'd like to show you that side of me in more ways than one. So, how about we get out of here?"

I slowly picked up my dirty martini from the bar and sipped it while putting a look of consideration on my face like I was really weighing his proposition. I knew that in his mind, him being a 6'5", two hundred ninety pound football player for the Washington Commanders guaranteed that I'd leave this bar with him. Not to mention the fact that this particular watering hole was known for having some of the best high-class escorts in the city. I knew that my tight, red, micro dress and matching red stilettos had caught his eye, but my body was what sold the dream. I was 5'0", weighing one hundred thirty-four pounds, with an ass that made men and women scream. My butter toffee complexion, firm titties, and beauty patent smile were just the right combination that made my thirty years seem younger while making me irresistible to any man's sin. The nigga standing in front of me was a case in point. Deep down, he really thought that he'd been seducing, but the reality was that he was the one caught in my web about to make a delicious meal.

"I came with my girls, and I'm the one driving," I said, sounding disappointed and reluctant at the same time.

"You can just leave your car with them and ride with me."

"Leave them bitches with my Bentley? I don't think so, but I've got a better idea. Why don't we all come with you?" I suggested.

The way that his eyes got huge told me that I'd just made his night in all the best possible ways.

"I'm with that. How many of your girls are with you?"

My response to his question was to look down the length of the bar and wave at my bitch, Skylar. She immediately slid off of the bar stool, rising to her full 5'11", one hundred fifty pounds, while pulling her little black dress down over her juicy ass and thick thighs. She was by far the baddest white chick I'd run across on my travels, and her natural fire red hair perfectly matched her temperament. Following her movement, my dark-skinned cousin, Tasha, aka Tink, got up and headed in our direction as well. Niggas loved Tink because she was what they called 'fun size', and that was a turn on for a lot of people. Shit, she got equal —_if not more —_love from women due to her 4'9", one hundred five pounds because she was the girly type who never looked bad in anything that she had on. The way that her short, snakeskin skirt, matching halter top, and white cowgirl boots had all types of heads turning as she walked toward us was proof. I waited until they were standing beside me before I made the introductions.

"Michael, this is Tink and Skylar. Ladies, this is..."

"Michael Newcome, starting quarterback for the Washington Commanders, lead MVP candidate, and the newly minted $70 million dollar a year man," Tink said, sounding very much like a schoolgirl with a crush.

I couldn't tell if Michael was blushing or simply flustered from her flattery, but his alabaster skin had definitely received a sudden infusion of color.

"I can see that someone is a fan," he said proudly.

"We all are... We're *big* fans," Skylar said, continuing the round of ego stroking we'd engaged in.

Michael was rich because his real money came from the endorsement deals that he'd had since he was a five-star recruit playing for Clemson, but he wasn't the flashy type of rich. Based on the deep dive I'd done into his background, I knew that he was wealthy because he didn't blow his money on frivolous shit, and neither did his wife, Margot. They both had diversified portfolios, they invested wisely, and they didn't spoil their only son nor their extended families. By all accounts, Michael didn't have a vise —_well, except for the fact that he treated his penis like community dick. Luckily for me and mine, this was the only flaw that we needed in order to exploit.

"So, are you ladies up for a little partying back at my place?" he asked.

"You must've read my mind," Skylar replied, smiling seductively.

"Let's go," I said, sitting my glass down and looping my arm through his.

The grin that spread across his face almost made me laugh out loud uncontrollably because I knew that this night was going down as one in the 'win' column for him, but little did he know, he'd fumbled the bag. We'd help him by picking that bitch up and running with it though. He led us outside to a navy-blue Lamborghini truck where he did the gentlemanly thing and opened the passenger side door for me.

"You all follow us," I said, tossing Tink my keys as I slid onto the smooth butterscotch leather seat.

Once he shut the door and hurried around to the driver side to get behind the wheel, we pulled off fast. I knew that I didn't have to worry about him losing my girls because we'd already put an Apple AirTag under his bumper before making our way into the bar.

"So, where are we headed?" I asked.

"You ever seen the inside of a mansion?"

"No, I can't say that I have," I lied, smiling convincingly.

"Well, you're in for a treat because we're headed to one."

"Oh, wow," I said, oozing with fake excitement, as I slyly kept my eyes on the side mirror.

My white Bentley Azure was keeping pace just fine, but I still slid my phone discreetly out of my Gucci clutch purse and sent a message so that they would know we were headed into Maryland. The research that we'd done on Mr. Newcome revealed that his East Coast mansion was in Maryland, he kept a penthouses in lower Manhattan, and he had an even bigger mansion in Montana that came with one hundred thirty acres of land. Real estate was part of Michael's portfolio, but only a few of his other properties interested me.

"So, uh, how much is this night of fun gonna cost me?" he asked, placing his hand on my left thigh.

Only through sheer force of will and practice did I keep from breaking at least six bones in this muthafucka's hand, but anyone who saw the smile on my face wouldn't have guessed that.

"It won't be cheap, baby, but I promise you that it'll be well worth it," I replied, snaking my hand in between him and my thigh while maneuvering to get to his zipper.

I wasted no time using my nimble fingers to render his zipper useless and give his dick room to breathe by freeing it from his pants and boxers. It only took seconds to have him fully hard and quite literally losing control as the SUV swerved, but he regained his composure enough to keep us traveling in a straight line.

"Let's see how good your concentration is," I said, pulling my hand back so that I could spit in it, and then, I grabbed his dick again.

I'd been told on more than one occasion, by more than one person, just how soft my hands were despite the firmness of my grip. With painful slowness, I stroked his dick like I loved it above all else in this world, and I could tell by the struggling breaths coming from his mouth that I was killing him. When the SUV swerved again, I tightened my grip and began moving my hand up and down faster.

"Stay focused," I whispered, leaning closer to him.

"I'm t-trying," he growled through clenched teeth.

I sped up my rhythm some more, and suddenly, his foot got heavier on the gas pedal, causing us to rocket forward.

"Are you ready, Michael?"

"N-no... yes!" he stammered, sounding torn between his wants and his needs.

I showed no mercy when I again increased the speed of my hand, causing a loud repetitive popping sound to echo throughout the SUV as my spit acted like jailhouse grease.

"Oh, God," he moaned, shaking hard enough to make him quickly put the truck on cruise control.

As soon as he let go of the wheel, his cum shot out into the darkness. Some of it coated the back of my hand like the daily moisturizer that I applied, but I didn't care because my mission of turning him out was closer to being accomplished.

"Do you feel better?" I asked.

"Fuck no! Now, I can't wait to get inside you and your friends because that second nut is gonna take longer to come."

"I wouldn't be so sure about that because we know a few different tricks that you might not be ready for," I replied, holding my hand up so that he could see it.

I waited until I knew that he was focused on his cum that was dripping down my knuckles, and then, I slowly brought my hand to my mouth and licked it clean like a big cat.

"Damn, is that how you feel?"

"I guess you'll have to wait and see," I replied teasingly.

Nothing else had to be said because he took the truck off of cruise and pushed the pedal to the floor until the speedometer hit one hundred ten miles per hour.

"Don't get us pulled over, superstar," I warned.

My words were ignored, but the result was that we were pulling up to his mansion twenty minutes later with my Bentley in tow. Michael and I got out and waited for Skylar and Tink to join us by his ride.

"Follow me, ladies, follow me," he said with barely contained excitement.

He led the way up to the front door where he entered using his palm print and a key code, and then, we followed him into the foyer.

"I know that you ladies like to handle the business before pleasure, so just give me a price, and we can get that part out of the way."

We all laughed at what he said, causing him to join in even though he didn't know why. Only we knew that what we found funny wouldn't be amusing to him in the slightest.

"How about a drink before we start crunching numbers?" I suggested.

"You're right. Where are my manners? Let's step into the living room since there's a bar in there," he suggested, leading the way deeper into the house.

Just off to the left of the foyer was a massive living room, and on the far wall was the bar.

"What would you all like to drink?"

"Champagne," Tink replied.

"Coming right up," he said, heading across the room.

While he was distracted, I gave Tink and Skylar a nod, and they immediately stripped their clothes off until all they wore was a mysterious smile.

I grabbed a bottle of clear liquid out of my purse and tucked it into my bra along with my phone before sitting the purse down. When Michael turned back around, he damn near dropped the bottle of champagne, along with the glasses, but luckily, I was right there to help out.

"Why don't you let me handle this while you, uh, quarterback that play over there?" I suggested, nodding at his living fantasy.

He passed me everything that he was holding without objection and began to shed his clothing while crossing the room. I moved back to the bar where I poured three glasses of champagne and dropped four liquid drops of fentanyl from the vial in my bra into the one intended for him. By the time I got over to the couch, Michael was in the middle of a sandwich hot enough to make the devil sweat. Tink was working her way across his chiseled chest using her tongue and lips, while Skylar was sucking his dick like she was trying to pull every secret out of him through the hole in the tip. I put the glasses on the table and then stepped to the side so that I could pull my phone out and film the play by play. My girls knew the drill, so they worked their angles just right. When Skylar popped the dick out of her mouth, the positions changed with the efficiency of an Indy pit crew, and Skylar was licking his neck while Tink hopped on the dick reverse cowgirl style. I made sure to catch this view from all angles because Tink was giving me *face*, and anybody watching would've sworn that Big Michael Newcome was knocking her loose with ten inches at least. By my estimate, he was probably seven inches on a good day, but my bitches could sell it like no other.

"Champagne time," I said, discretely pointing to the glass that I wanted Tink to give him.

She hopped off the dick at the same time that Skylar backed away, which left him looking comically sexually frustrated and bewildered.

"Drink up," Tink said, putting the glass to his lips and tilting it.

There was no hesitation in the way that he guzzled the beverage, but the ladies took their time sipping from their glasses.

"I-I need somebody to get back on this thing because it hurts," he said, grabbing his dick and wagging it at us.

"Patience, Mr. Quarterback, we've got all night. Your wife is out of town, right?" I asked.

"Yep, she sure is... Now come on and let's have some real fun," he replied, standing up.

When he attempted to take a step forward, he stumbled, and that forced him to plant his naked ass back on his white leather couch.

"You okay?" I asked, giving Tink and Skylar a knowing look as I lowered the phone in my hand.

"Yeah, I'm-I'm... fine," he slurred, lying his head back on the couch like the weight of it was too much for his neck.

I winked at my girls, and then, I headed back toward the foyer and outside to my car. I retrieved a black duffel bag from the trunk, and then I headed back inside to finish the job. By the time I got back, it was obvious that Michael was barely conscious even though his dick was still rock hard.

"I mean, damn, I hate to waste good wood like this," Tink said.

"How much did you give him, Kyn?" Skylar asked.

"Look, that's a big muthafuckin white boy, and if he were to suddenly become lucid while we're setting the stage or pulling off the job, then we'd have to kill him. So, I gave his ass enough to keep him nodding for a little while. Don't trip. We'll be long gone by morning," I assured her.

"Can I finish him off real quick?" Tink asked.

"Man, hurry up, ho," I said, screwing my face up at her even though I wasn't mad for real.

She just laughed as she jumped back on the dick like it was her favorite tricycle bicycle. By the time I got my phone back up to film it, she had both hands on that nigga's shoulders, and she was riding that dick like a jockey in the Kentucky Derby. The way that his head was bouncing around, and the fact that he was moaning passionately, made it impossible to tell that he was high out of his mind. When he palmed both of her ass cheeks, I knew that he was definitely feeling the pressure she was putting on him with that good pussy.

"Get it, cuz, make that million-dollar dick spit up inside you," I said, laughing and encouraging her bullshit.

Tink took directions like a porn star, and before I knew

it, she was popping that pussy loud enough to make a bitch look around for gunshots.

"Ahhh," he groaned weakly.

"Fuck-fuck, dammit!" Tink growled.

Skylar and I watched in amazement as she rode that dick until he passed out.

"Bitch, if he's dead, then your pussy is gonna be more famous than ten serial killers," Skylar said, laughing.

"Shit, it-it already is," Tink panted, climbing off the now limp dick.

"We've got work to do. Let's get to it," I said, passing Skylar the duffle bag.

Her and Tink unloaded the guns, drugs, and cash, making sure to spread everything out all over the coffee table. There was meth and a meth pipe, heroin, percs, and an obviously used cut soda straw. Once those props were set up just right, Tink and Skylar rolled Michael onto his stomach, and then, Tink put the twelve-inch, black strap on around her waist so that it hung down in front of her pussy.

She climbed on top of Michael, and once she had the head of the strap on in between his taunt ass cheeks, I lifted my phone again.

"Now, Michael, just remember to relax because we don't want you to shit all over the place like last time," Tink said.

With her rehearsed line delivered, I lowered the phone again, and she climbed off of him.

"Alright, let's get to work," I said.

Tink took the strap-on off, and then, they quickly put their clothes back on. While they were doing that, I wandered through the house to find the dining room, and then, I brought a chair back from there into the living room. It took all three of us to get his big ass in the chair and zip tie him in place, but when that was done, the hard part was over.

"Let's clean house. Pack the Bentley and the Lamborghini truck, no junk, just value," I said.

"Got it," Skylar said.

"Got it," Tink chimed in.

We split up to cover the massive eight-bedroom mansion, and it took us three hours, but we managed to grab about four million in art and jewelry. That was nothing compared to what we'd come for though. After we packed the vehicles, we returned to the living room where I administered a shot of Narcan straight to Michael's heart.

"What happened?" he asked, gasping like he'd just returned from the dead.

"I'll give you the short version," I said, holding up my phone and pressing play on the video I'd made.

The expression on his face went from death, to sickly, to defeated.

"What do you want?" he asked.

"Well, since I know that you know how damaging this will be to your personal life, to say nothing of that guaranteed contract you signed, I think asking for full ownership of MILLIONDOLLARBOY LLC is a reasonable demand," I replied.

"But that's-that's my company. My real estate company."

"I'm aware. You own two Malibu beach houses sitting side by side on the water's edge, a place in the Hamptons, and a penthouse in Dubai under that LLC. By my guess, that's worth..."

I turned and looked at Skylar, who had the necessary paperwork for Michael to sign.

"That's about $107 million in a soft market," Skylar said.

I could see the will to fight in his eyes, but my response was to simply hold up my phone again, and defeat rushed back to contorting his features.

"Where do I sign?" he mumbled.

"On pages six and seven. I'll be your notary this evening," Skylar replied, smiling.

3

JAKWAN

Los Angeles, CA
One Week Later

"How can I help you today, sir?"

I put my best business smile on my face while approaching the cute, short, blonde hair sales lady.

"I'm in the market for a new watch. Nothing too gaudy but nothing so commonplace that my mailman might have the same one tucked away in his sock drawer," I replied.

"I understand perfectly. My name is Bethany, and I'll be the one to service you today. Are you a collector, or will this be for you to wear as a functional piece?"

"Actually, I'm a little bit of both, so why don't you show me something in both categories?" I suggested.

"Excellent idea, sir. I'll be right back," she replied, backing away from the counter and disappearing into the back of the jewelry store.

While I waited, I decided to check out the inventory

they kept in different locked cases throughout the store. I was here for pleasure and not business, but my brain was crunching numbers on each piece that I looked at like I was about to pull an old school smash and grab. An engagement ring caught my eye, forcing me to stop and take a closer look.

"She'll love it," a sultry voice said from over my shoulder.

When I looked to my right, I got an unexpected eyeful of a beautiful brown skinned woman rocking an off-white Black Billionaire linen dress with flesh colored undergarments hugging her voluptuous curves. I tried not to stare at her body too long because I wasn't trying to come off as a weird nigga, but by the time I actually made eye contact with her hazel green stare, I knew that I was in trouble.

"Uh, excuse me?" I asked, still confused by her comment.

"I said that she'll love it. I saw you looking at the four-carat, princess cut, diamond engagement ring with the emerald accents, and it's a great choice for your soon to be fiancée. She'll definitely say yes."

The smile that accompanied her words was just as intoxicating as the rest of her, but it was her quick appraisal of the jewelry that intrigued me more than her beauty.

"You've got a good eye... but I wasn't looking at it for a woman," I replied.

"Oh... well then, that must've sounded like the worst pickup line ever," she said, laughing genuinely.

I laughed with her while shaking my head.

"Nah, not even close, trust me. I've said some corny shit to try and holla at women when I was younger."

"Oh, really? And what do you say now?" she asked flirtatiously.

Her question caused me to turn toward her fully so that she could see the fact that I was now completely engaged in the conversation.

"These days, I just keep it simple because less is more. So, I'll say... Hi, my name is Jakwan, and you are?" I asked, extending my hand to her.

She smiled and bit her lip in a cute, self-conscious way before sticking her hand out to take mine.

"I'm Kyndra."

"Nice to meet you," I said, reminding myself not to hold on to her hand for too long.

I didn't know if it was bad luck or great timing, but the sales lady returned carrying two boxes in her hand and pulled up to the side of the counter where we stood.

"Okay, so I have two choices that I think you will find to your standards. Here's the first one from the Black Billionaire limited edition collection. It's rose gold with diamonds and rubies in the face and throughout the band. It gives you three different time zones simultaneously. The second one that I have for you is a presidential Rolex covered in diamonds set in platinum."

I inspected both watches without touching them, again doing the numbers in my mind just because it was like mental exercise.

"I'd go with the limited edition Black Billionaire," Kyndra said from beside me.

"Explain please," I said, looking at Kyndra, intrigued by what was to come out of her mouth.

"Well, first off, Black Billionaire is Black-owned, and

it's always good to support our people. Beyond that though, the value of the limited edition will appreciate more than the Rolex. Rolex is no longer popular with rappers and urban culture, so it's lost a lot of its desirability. Old, rich, white men still cling to it as a status symbol, but Jay-Z is a billionaire, and he ain't rocked a Rolex in years. The limited edition is also about $5K less than the Rolex."

I looked at Bethany, who was trying to discreetly check the price, and I could tell by the surprised expression that she wore that Kyndra's price point was spot on. This made me laugh out loud.

"Well, Bethany, you heard the lady. So, I'll take the Black Billionaire limited edition," I said, pulling out my wallet and extracting my Black Amex card.

"Very good, sir. And can I help you with anything, Miss?" Bethany asked, looking at Kyndra.

"I'll meet you over by that case," Kyndra said, pointing to a row of diamond necklaces opposite the counter we were at.

When Kyndra moved off, I slyly signaled Bethany to add another item to my purchase list by pointing at it, and then I moved over to where Kyndra was standing.

"She'll love it," I said softly.

"Say what?"

"I said she'll love it. I see you eyeing that diamond studded choker, which looks to be about thirty to thirty-five square cut VVS stones set in platinum," I replied.

"I see that I'm not the only one with a good eye, but what makes you think that it's for another woman? It could simply be for me."

"You're right; it could. I was just fishing to see if

anyone, male or female, was occupying your time," I said, smiling shamelessly.

"Ah, I see. Well, for the record, I'm a *huge* fan of dick despite my ability to appreciate a woman's beauty and softness. More importantly though, my time is precious, so I only choose to give those who are worthy access to those moments."

"Understood and respected. I admire a woman who understands her value and carries herself accordingly because only then can she make the world respect the crown that she wears," I replied.

"Spoken like a true king," she said, smiling at me.

The look that we shared lasted long enough for me to feel the energy of reciprocated interest, but before a move could be made to capitalize on it, good ole Bethany returned.

"Here you are, Mr. Riley. Your receipt is in the bag," she said, handing me my credit card back as she pushed the bag across the counter toward me.

I took it and looked inside of it to find two boxes, one bigger than the other. Kyndra's attention was on the diamond choker that Bethany was pulling out to show her, which gave me a moment to discreetly remove the smaller box from the bag.

"Thanks for all your help, Kyndra. Maybe I'll see you around sometime," I said.

"Maybe," she replied, giving me that gorgeous smile again.

I slid the ring box in front of her as I grabbed my bag and stepped around her, headed for the door.

"What's this?" she called after me.

"Just a token of my appreciation for your beauty and your time," I replied over my shoulder without pausing in stride.

I didn't stay to see her reaction because the gift wasn't really given with an expected response. I just did it because I could and because, deep down, I knew that a woman like that deserved the precious jewels to match her beauty. I climbed behind the wheel of the black-on-black Ferrari SUV I'd purchased yesterday and quickly slipped into traffic as I headed back to the hotel. By the time I'd gotten to the penthouses I'd rented out at the Four Seasons, my mind was off Kyndra and back on the reason that I was in the City of Angels to begin with.

"What did it look like?" Blaze asked as soon as I came through the door.

"The gallery that the jewelry will be displayed at is heavily fortified. We're still at least six hours away from the exhibit kicking off, but there are already sentries posted in the front and back of the building, and they were armed," I replied.

"So, it's like I said," Jayson commented from his position on one of the two couches in the living room.

"It's exactly as you said, but I didn't do my own recon because I doubted your ability to assess the situation. I wanted to see what ideas I had that could work with yours once we all sat down to strategize. Everybody, let's pull up in the living room," I replied, headed in that direction.

I took a seat in one of the overstuffed chairs closest to the balcony, and I waited for Blaze and Fabian to join us. Once we were all gathered around, the strategy session began.

"There's gonna be big attendance opening night, including a huge celebrity presence because we're in LA LA Land," Fabian said.

"Do we know whose jewelry collection it is that's gonna be on display?" I asked.

"No, and the mystery behind it all is what's gassing the number of people wanting to attend. The A-list celebrities in this town believe that they'll know the jewels and their owner at first sight," Jayson replied.

"What have you learned through the back channels?" I asked, looking at Fabian for an answer.

"Only that the prince of Saudi Arabia has something to do with this, which means that it could be from his private collection," Fabian replied.

"He's not on the guest list," Jayson said.

"True, but if they *are* his jewels, then we know that the value won't be anything less than nine figures," Fabian added.

We all got quiet as that amount sank in because when it came to playing for big money like this, we had to make damn sure that all of our bases were covered.

"What's our way in?" I asked.

"You and Jayson are already on the guest list as the reputable businessmen/owners of the top exotic car dealerships on the East Coast. Your legal net worth allows you to play in this arena. As for Blaze, well, whatever his way in will be the same way that the jewels come out," Fabian replied.

"You got an idea, Blaze?" I asked.

"Well, based on the schematics Fabian pulled up, I

figure that we're gonna either have to attack from above or below."

"Are you volunteering to brave the infamous LA sewer system?" Jayson asked.

"Shit, for this type of money, I'd go through the Mexican sewer system," Blaze replied seriously.

We all laughed because we knew that, without a doubt, that nigga meant what he was saying.

"Going underground might be the best play. Jayson, what do you think?" I asked.

He pondered the question for a few moments before responding.

"It's the move but with a slight twist though, which means that we need to get started now," he replied.

He quickly explained the twist, and we all nodded in agreement.

"Meeting adjourned," I said, standing up.

Now that we all knew what we needed to do and what our window of opportunity was, we got down to the business that we loved the most. To each of us, robbery was an art form similar to a seduction that came with its own orgasmic feeling during the planning stages —_almost like foreplay before actual penetration. There was no high like it to be found in the world, which made it more than an addiction for each of us. As I went into my room to take a shower and get ready, my mind drifted toward something else that I wanted to be addicted to. Actually, it was someone. My instincts told me that Kyndra was different from any woman I'd ever known, fucked, or fucked over, and that made her an intriguing mystery that I wanted to solve.

Tonight, my focus would have to be on business, but

once this mission was complete, I was most definitely gonna find out who Kyndra was and what she was all about. I jumped in the shower and then made myself presentable in a tailored, cream Black Billionaire suit with a white button up shirt open at the collar and no tie. The only piece of jewelry that I wore was the watch that I'd purchased a few hours ago, which again made my thoughts turn to Kyndra. I forcefully put those aspirations into the back of my mind, making sure to lock the door on the fifty shades of gray, and went to meet up with my niggas to go over the last-minute details. Blaze had already left because he needed the head start. Nothing needed to be added to the plan, and Fabian was gonna work his magic from the hotel where he'd already hacked into the gallery's security system. He had three monitors which were feeding him thirty-six different camera angles, so he'd be the all-knowing and all seeing. After Jayson and I grabbed our encrypted phones from him, we went downstairs to the restaurant in the hotel to grab a bite to eat in order to kill some time. An hour and a half later, we were walking through the door of the Honey Drips gallery, and the curtain was officially up on the show.

"Work the room," I said to Jayson before heading off in the opposite direction.

My pace of movement was slow, as was most patrons with a keen eye who were moving from display to display. It wasn't until I came across a 16th century, solid gold, African crown accented with diamonds, emeralds, and rubies strategically placed to resemble a headband just above the bottom lip of the crown itself that I paused. Never had I seen a piece more gorgeous, and I was quite certain that it had never been on display anywhere in the world before now. There was no information on the plain white card that was sitting in front of it, which led me to believe that even its owner didn't know its origins.

"It's beautiful, isn't it? I'd put it at about late 15th, early 16th, century Africa, undoubtedly from the Ashanti kingdom because they were notorious for their gold crafts-manship before the race for Africa and the Europeans tried to enslave the entire continent," she said.

For a few moments, I simply continued to stare at the crown before us, trying to gather my scattered thoughts, but then I turned to face her.

"You've got a great eye, Kyndra. But you already knew that, didn't you?"

4

KYNDRA

"I've been told that I have a great eye, but for reasons that I can't fathom, it sounds different coming from you," I replied.

His fixed gaze drank me in from my jade green, six-inch, Gucci heels, up the matching green, Valentino dress that stopped just above my knees and hugged me closer than any lover, until his eyes finally reached mine. When spotting him from across the room, I'd done excellent with concealing my surprise and the physical heat that seeing him again caused, but now that we were this close, I could feel the blush rising from my neck.

"You look absolutely stunning," he said in a low tone that was like sonic waves to my pussy's wetness.

"You clean up damn good yourself, but I'm sure that you already know that."

"Hearing it come from you makes it hit different," he replied, smiling seductively.

Even if I'd wanted to stop the grin that was spreading across my face, I knew that I couldn't. And truthfully, I didn't want to. In my mind, I knew that I was here on business, but there was no reason that this handsome, chocolate man couldn't be the necessary distraction to go along with work.

"So, were you scheduled to attend this event tonight prior to our fortunate run in earlier, or did you come here looking for me?"

"Well, I prefer to think that it's fate at work for a multitude of reasons, but no matter what, I'm glad that we happened to be in the same place at the same time," he replied.

"As am I because, now, I get to ask you a $75,000 question," I said, holding up my hand for him to see the engagement ring he'd so casually given me earlier.

"It matches your outfit and your eyes perfectly."

"I'm very aware of that, Jakwan, thank you. But what is the meaning behind it?"

"Please call me Kwan, and the meaning should be obvious. A beautiful ring for a gorgeous woman," he replied smoothly.

"Is this your idea of keeping it simple? Because this looks like the full court press from where I'm sitting."

"Oh, no, sweetheart, this is nowhere *near* the full court press," he said, smiling devilishly.

My brain was screaming, *oh, lawd*, because there was no doubt that this negro right here was dangerous, but now wasn't the time or place to ride this ride. My daddy had taught me better.

"Here you go, cuz. I brought you a glass of champagne," Tink said, suddenly appearing beside us with two glasses in her hands.

"Uh, th-thanks, cuz," I replied, trying to hide the fact that I was flustered as a muthafucka.

I took the glass that she offered and quickly sipped some of the cool liquid to quench the rising heat in my throat.

"Hi, I'm Tink," she said, holding her free hand out in front of her.

"Nice to meet you, Tink. I'm Kwan," he replied, taking her hand and kissing the back of it softly.

"Kwan, as in... Jakwan?" she asked, looking at me without letting his hand go.

The smile on his face suddenly got wider, and the feeling of heat that I'd been in a death match with started to spread throughout my body.

"So, you've heard of me?" he asked, trying to make it sound like an innocent question.

"Yeah. You've got some amazing cars, and I was thinking about upgrading to a Rolls Royce truck," Tink said, omitting the fact that we'd definitely talked about his fine ass and the ring he'd bought me.

"Just tell me what dealership you're closest to, and I'll make sure that you can take it off the lot by tomorrow morning," he assured her.

"Oh, it's like that?" Tink asked.

"Try me," he replied with ease.

"Okay... I'll be in Elizabeth, New Jersey by tomorrow. How long will it take you to get the truck there?" she asked.

His eyes shifted from hers to mine, and he stared at me

for a few moments with an expression that I couldn't quite read. Then, he suddenly looked away and motioned for someone to come here. A few seconds later, an attractive brother with almond brown skin, neat, straight back cornrows in his hair, and an obviously nice build beneath his tailored suit pulled up on us.

"This is my brother, Jayson. Jayson, this is Kyndra and her cousin, Tink."

"Ladies," Jayson said, shaking both of our hands politely.

"Tink wants the newest Rolls Royce truck in Elizabeth, New Jersey by tomorrow. Can it be done?" Kwan asked.

"Just tell me what color you want and what extras you need," Jayson replied without hesitation.

"I, uh, I don't know. I hadn't thought that far ahead," Tink admitted, smiling sheepishly.

"That's okay. Why don't we grab you another glass of champagne, and we can go over the particulars while enjoying the rest of the exhibit?" Jayson suggested, offering her his arm.

The bitch didn't even bother to look at me and check to find out if I was okay alone with Kwan. She just took the arm offered, and in a flash, they disappeared.

"Do I make you nervous, Kyndra?"

"No. Why would you ask me that?" I countered, feeling slightly self-conscious.

"Just my curiosity getting the best of me, I guess. Would you like to explore the rest of the rare jewels on display?"

Something about the way that he asked that question

made the hairs on the back of my neck stand up, but it wasn't like sensing danger or anything. It was more of a thrill. The only thing that I didn't like was the imbalance that I felt around this man. He unsettled me, and that was a foreign feeling because I was used to being the one who ruffled a nigga's feathers. Here I was, wearing a fucking engagement ring that this man bought me, like I belonged to him or something, and that wasn't how the game went. It was time to flip the script.

"There's a rare piece that I'd love to show you, but it's not on display to the public. Only serious collectors and investors can see it, but I'll make an exception for you," I said.

Before he could respond, I sat my glass down, took him by the hand, and led him to the back of the gallery. I'd memorized the blueprint layout of the entire place, so I knew that there were three offices and an appraisal room in the back away from the gallery floor. I chose the first office that I came to, pulled him inside, and locked the door behind us. He looked around, confused at first, and then he stared at me, clearly questioning my motives and intentions. My actions spoke for me as I stepped up to him, grabbed him by a fistful of his suit jacket, and pulled him toward me. His head dipped like our lips were magnetized and drawn to each other, and the next thing that either of us knew, we were kissing. The first taste of his tongue brought forward the lioness aggression in me, and I pulled out all the stops when it came to the power of my mouth's seduction. While the magic worked within our mouths, my hands were pulling my dress up over my ass and my hips, and I was secretly thankful that I decided not to wear panties tonight. I unzipped his slacks and pulled his dick out, and then, I pulled him by it to the desk in the corner.

"H-hold up, K-Kyndra. We can't..."

"We can, and we are. So, it's either we're fucking or I'm fucking," I said, looking at him in a deadly serious way.

I didn't have time to brace before he lifted me off of my feet and put my little ass on the desk, but my legs spread for him without the need of a conscious thought.

"Kwan," I moaned, as he pushed what felt like at least nine inches of hard dick inside me with one swift move.

My body curled around his like a hungry boa constrictor, and my arms were wrapped around his neck for leverage. With every stroke that he delivered, I was lifting into him, letting him feel all of the pussy power that I possessed.

"Shit," he growled, struggling to find a rhythm that didn't make him tremble with the desire to climax.

I could feel the raw power radiating through and around his body, and it made my pussy's grip put a strangle hold on the dick the deeper that he dove into me. With each stroke, I heard my pussy juices talking louder, and I could feel my body disintegrating under his touch in the best possible ways. All of a sudden, he stopped in mid stroke with a concerned look replacing the passion that had been contorting his face and clouding his vision.

"Do you smell smoke?" he asked breathlessly.

"Wh-what?"

"Smoke? Do you smell smoke?" he asked again.

At first, I thought that he was playing or that this was some new kind of dirty talk, but the look on his face was too serious. The screaming sound of the fire alarm drowned out whatever I was gonna say and effectively fucked up the mood because, suddenly, I couldn't feel all that good dick throbbing within my walls.

"We gotta go," he said, fixing his clothes and then lifting me off the desk.

I quickly pulled my dress back down and ran my fingers through my hair to smooth it out just in case it was out of place. My body was burning up with the need for complete fulfillment, but I forcefully pushed those thoughts from my mind because it wasn't just the fire alarm screaming now. I could hear voices raising outside the door somewhere, and I could definitely smell smoke. This wasn't a drill. This shit was serious, and it had royally fucked up my plans.

"I gotta find my cousin," I said, hurrying toward the door.

The speed of his arm shooting out and the force of his grip startled me and caused me to pull up short.

"Stay behind me because we don't know what's going on out there," he said, stepping in front of me like a human shield.

His chivalrous side had that bass back beating with a vengeance in between my still damp thighs, but I managed to focus on what was more important —_getting to Tink. When he opened the door, the noise level raised to a fever pitch, and I could taste the panic with the same intensity that I had the sex that had been in the air. Kwan stepped out into the hall with my hand grasped tightly in his, and I followed his lead.

"Please exit quickly and calmly, ladies and gentlemen. There's no need to panic," a voice boomed over the gallery's loudspeaker.

People were following directions, but I could feel their desire to do a mad dash to safety.

"Kyndra!"

I looked left at the sound of my name being called, and when I saw Tink headed toward me, my heart flooded with relief. The way that she ran into my arms reminded me of when she used to have nightmares when we were kids, and I held her now like I had then.

"You okay?" I asked.

"Yeah, but Skylar said that the roof is on fire. Literally," Tink replied.

I knew that Skylar had the best view in the house because she was staked out in a Sprinter van across the street from the gallery.

"Where's Jayson?" Kwan asked.

"I don't-I don't know. We got separated. He led me to the front door and told me to get out while he went back to look for you two," Tink replied, sounding distressed.

When I looked at Kwan, I saw the concern on his face, and it created a feeling in me that I couldn't describe.

"You two need to get out *now*, and I'll find Jayson," Kwan said.

His tone left no room for argument, but I liked that type of gangsta shit. I stepped away from Tink and toward him for a second.

"I'm not done with you, so you better not get yourself

killed," I demanded, pulling him toward me and kissing him fast and hard.

"Trust me, this is only the beginning," he assured me once I'd pulled back.

I nodded because I didn't trust my voice, and then, I grabbed my cousin's hand so that we wouldn't get separated. We began to weave our way quickly through the crowd, and a few moments later, I was able to pull some much needed, cool, fresh air into my lungs. You would've thought that the people fleeing the event would've thought to get as far away as possible, but instead they were standing back a few feet and watching the flames rising higher from the roof. For a second, I found myself doing the same shit, but then, I felt Tink pulling me toward the Sprinter van, and I was able to refocus.

"We need to get out of here before the cops show up," Skylar said as soon as she opened the side door.

"What are we running for? It's not like we actually pulled the robbery off or got caught doing something, so we're good," I replied, climbing into the back with Tink.

"We're good? I know that your ass ain't crazy enough to think that we can still pull this heist off... So, what's the real reason that you ain't trying to leave?" Skylar asked.

Tink immediately started to giggle, and I quickly popped her ass in the head to shut her up.

"Shut up, bitch. I just wanna make sure that they got out safely," I replied defensively.

"They? Who the fuck is 'they', and is *that* why you smell freshly fucked?" Skylar asked, smirking.

Tink's giggles turned into certified laughter, but she was smart enough to move before I could pop her ass again.

"I'm not even gonna dignify that question with a response, and if you smelling pussy, it might be your upper lip," I replied, taking a seat and looking out the window at the action unfolding.

I could feel both women wanting to press me for details, but they wisely kept their mouths shut. My eyes stayed glued to the front doors of the gallery, but there was still no sight of Kwan or Jayson yet. When Tink took the seat next to mine and began watching with me, I didn't feel so thirsty. A few minutes later, the fire trucks came roaring up the block, and firefighters hopped out like ants at a picnic, ready to work. Based on the look of things, I thought it would be a wild ride for them to get the fire under control and keep it from spreading, but within fifteen minutes, there was nothing left of the flames except for thick smoke.

There didn't look to be any structural damage, but I was more concerned with Kwan's safety.

"I don't see 'em," Tink said.

I didn't say anything because I was worried that the fear would creep into my voice. It wasn't until I saw the cops pull up in mass that my fear was replaced by curiosity, and I found myself opening the van door.

"What are you doing?" Skylar asked.

"Just stay here. I'll be right back," I replied.

I headed back across the street and stopped the first cop I came to.

"Officer, I was working inside the gallery this evening, and I left my personal items in there when the evacuation was ordered. Will I be able to retrieve them tonight?"

"I'm sorry, ma'am, but no one is allowed inside. It's a crime scene."

"But you don't know that the fire wasn't accidental, so why…"

"The fire wasn't the crime, ma'am; it was the distraction. The robbery was the crime," he replied, walking away.

5

KWAN

New York
Three Days Later

"It might be time for a vacation," Jayson said, putting down the tablet he'd been holding when I walked in the kitchen.

"Oh, yeah? Where are we going, and what's the target?"

"There is no target, and we're going somewhere that no one would think to look for us," he replied.

I'd been in the process of fixing myself a cup of coffee, but what he was saying, and the tone that he was saying it with, made me stop and turn from the kitchen counter to face him.

"What's up?" I asked.

"I found out whose jewels we stole."

"Okay. And?" I asked, not feeling any type of apprehension about whatever rich douche bag we robbed.

"The story about the Saudi Arabian prince was just a

smoke screen used to hide the real owner's identity. The real owner, or owners, is the triad."

I paused for a moment to consider what he was saying as a sudden burst of apprehension kicked in.

"The triad? As in the Chinese triad? Where the hell would they get that rare, priceless collection?" I asked skeptically.

"I don't know, but it makes sense why no one has seen any of it before now. It also makes sense why the bounty for information about the robbery was at $10 million dollars yesterday and has moved up to $100 million dollars today."

Hearing the astronomical jump in numbers made my eyebrows raise and my palms sweat a little. Offering up that much money told me just how valuable the collection was that we made disappear, but it also told me how high the stakes were now.

"A vacation doesn't seem like a bad idea, but how are we gonna sell the idea to Blaze and Fabian? You know that them niggas are workaholics," I said.

"I already talked to both of them, and they're already packing their shit."

Again, the wave of apprehension swept over me because I knew how much my niggas loved their work, so typically taking some time off meant twisting their arms. That didn't sound like the case this time though, which told me that the threat was real, and the info was credible.

"We gotta clean house before we go. No loose ends," I said, looking him squarely in the eyes.

"Our associates are already on their way to receive their

cuts from the robbery. We've got about three hours before the meeting," he replied before picking the tablet back up.

As I went back to fixing my first cup of coffee, my mind began to race with details of what had brought us to this fork in the road. Aside from running into Kyndra and her cousin, the plan had gone smoothly, and we'd cleared the entire gallery out in under ten minutes. Dragging the U.S. military sacks full of loot through the sewer system wasn't exactly fun, but the payoff was worth it —_or at least it had seemed worth it before I woke up with a bounty on my head big enough to bring out the top hittas on every continent. The unanswered question that I had now was where exactly could one find safety from the Chinese triad.

"Any ideas about where we should relocate to?" I asked, turning back to Jayson.

"Well, I was thinking that Russia would be a good spot, but then I remembered that Putin is friends with the Chinese. So, that only leaves North Korea."

"Ain't no way in hell that you think our Black, nigga asses can blend in over there in North Korea," I said, chuckling.

"Blend in? Nah. We'll stand out as rich American businessmen though."

I could see how that would make us somewhat untouchable over there, but I also knew how unpredictable the dictator of North Korea could be.

"I think our best bet may be to hide in plain sight. We don't gotta move the stuff that we lifted from the gallery anytime soon, so all that we really have to do is make sure that our business associates don't get loose lips," I said.

When Jayson put the tablet down again and looked at me, I could see the contemplation about what I was saying.

"We'd only look guilty if we ran then," he replied.

"Exactly."

"I'll call Blaze and Fabian," he said, getting up and leaving the room.

I took my cup and headed back upstairs to my loft to take a quick shower. The loft was owned by our company and located in Manhattan, which allowed us to hide amongst crooked wealthy people after we pulled off particularly big licks. The move that we'd pulled off in L.A. was probably our biggest lick thus far for one stop shopping, but this wasn't the movies where we retired after a massive score. Our best move right now was to get back to work, only we would hit a different kind of target this time around. A deviation.

By the time I took a shower and threw some clothes on, I knew which direction we would head in, and I made a few calls while I was still in the bedroom. Once I had all of the info that was necessary, I selected a chrome Springfield XM .45 pistol from my wall safe, tucked it into the waist of my pants, and headed back downstairs. I found Jayson back on the bar stool in the kitchen with his tablet in his hands, checking the stock marker numbers.

"What did they say?" I asked, referring to Fabian and Blaze.

"We're all on the same page. Since we're not running though, what's our next move?"

"We've got some work to do in Kentucky. There's a syndicate of white boys out there pushing meth all across the state and into parts of Oklahoma and Kansas. My sources say that they clear about $30 million every couple weeks and wash the money in house through the local communities and farm lands," I replied.

"Sounds lucrative. Give me all the specifics so that I can have us battle ready and operational within the next forty-eight hours."

I took a seat on the bar stool across from him, and we began to plot a blow that would cripple the infrastructure of this Midwest syndicate.

We all loved the thrill of robbery, but when it came to hitting those with ill-gotten gains, it was more fun because the rules changed. Our preference was to not kill children, but our mandate was to leave no witnesses. This type of job with the syndicate allowed for our skills of finesse and brutality to coexist, and that was when we got to showcase our full potential. It took us a couple hours to put together something workable, and then, Jayson called Fabian to get the information we needed about who would be in charge of the money. They had several different stash houses but only two spots where they manufactured the meth out of, so we planned to hit everywhere at the same time.

"I think that we should use a biker gang called the Grim Reapers out of Lexington, Kentucky because they're rivals of this syndicate. They used to control the drug trade in Kentucky when it came to methamphetamine, but they were pushed out, and I'd bet that they weren't happy about it," he said.

"The enemy of my enemy is my friend, not my enemy."

"That's the idea. Do you want me to reach out to them?" he asked.

"Yeah, do it. Offer them their territory back and whatever dope they find in the stash houses to go along with ten percent of whatever we lift overall. Giving them all of that should make us friends and repeat customers should we require their services again."

"Okay, I'll get on it and..."

His phone started ringing, interrupting his statement, but I caught a look of surprise on his face.

"What is it?" I asked.

"It's a newly programmed number for Tink."

Hearing that name made my mind flash to Kyndra, and the taste of passion was instantly back on my tongue.

"Answer it," I said, curious as to how this would play out.

"Hello?" Jayson said, putting his phone on speaker and sitting it between us on the counter.

"It's good to know that you're alive, so I guess that I can cuss you and your brother out about my Rolls Royce truck," Tink said.

"No need to cuss anybody out, sweetheart. Don't forget that you were supposed to call me and confirm when you were ready to take delivery," Jayson replied.

"Then consider this your confirmation call. I'm back on the East Coast, in New Jersey, so when can I expect you to keep up your side of the agreement?" she asked.

The shift in her tone told me that I was missing parts from the conversation they'd had after leaving Kyndra and I, and the sudden smile on his face told me that I was right. He looked at his watch before glancing at me, and then, he grabbed his phone before quickly leaving the room. I had to laugh out loud at his sudden clandestine behavior, but the humor faded fast when my thoughts turned back to Kyndra.

After all that we'd shared in a day together, I didn't even walk away with her phone number. At the time, securing the bag seemed more important than anything else, but now, I was sitting here jealous of Jayson's wealth because he was still on the journey that money couldn't buy. I wasn't trying to convince myself that I was ready for love, or to build a life with Kyndra, but I had to admit that she was worth getting to know on a deeper level. That would have to wait until I had time to slow down in life though because right now, I needed to focus my energy in one direction. As if on cue, the doorbell to the loft rang, and I went to let our West Coast business associates in. After checking the camera by the door, I opened it to find two middle aged, reasonably fit, white men and one attractive white woman in her early thirties standing on my doorstep.

"Bill, Larry, Julia, thanks for making the trip on such short notice," I said, stepping back to let them enter the loft.

"It's our pleasure, especially since we're about to become richer than we'd ever dreamed," Larry replied, leading the way into the loft.

"We'll be meeting in the study to your right. I'm just waiting for Jayson to finish up his business call," I said, closing and locking the door once the last person entered.

I followed them into the study and waited until they were seated comfortably before I got down to what I really wanted from them.

"Before we get to the money, I need to know who all knows about me and my crew's involvement," I said, removing my pistol.

"Jakwan, what's the meaning of this?" Larry asked with righteous indignation filling his tone.

"This is what they call the price of doing business. So, if you wanna live a little longer, I suggest that you tell me who knows about our alliance," I replied, pulling the slide on the gun and chambering the first round.

"N-no one outside of this room knows of your involvement," Bill assured me.

The look of terror in his eyes made what he was saying believable, but I still knew that each of the people in the room with me was a liability. My loyalty was to me and mine, just like I was sure that their loyalty was to their family and the ones that they loved. That meant that if and when the wrong people came along with the right questions, the answers that were given would lead to the deaths of those that I loved. That made this math equation a real simple one.

"I'd like to personally thank each of you for the business that we've done over the years, but I think it's best that we go our separate ways," I said, raising the gun and aiming it at Larry.

"Wait, you don't have to..."

I silenced his plea with two shots to his face before turning my gun on his partners in crime. Bill actually made the valiant attempt to lunge at me, but the first round from the .45 put a nice size peephole in his forehead, allowing me to glimpse the moment that his brain functions ceased. Julia tried to run, and she actually made it to the study's entrance before Jayson popped around the corner with his black Glock .19 already up and trained. Julia tried to stop her forward momentum, but it was Jayson's two shots to the chest that reversed her body's motion and sent her flying backwards. When she hit the ground, I was standing over top of her in a flash, and I delivered the kill shot that ruined her pretty face.

"Damn, bruh, you couldn't wait for me?" he asked.

"Nigga, I didn't know how long you planned on being on the phone boo loving and shit. Business comes first."

"I'll remember that you said that," he replied, smirking before turning around to leave the room.

I disregarded him completely, tucked my pistol, and pulled out my phone to contact my people who knew how to make bodies disappear for a small fee. Once that was done, I went to the wall safe hidden in the study and removed $25K for the purposes of payment, and then, I set my focus on the details. First, I removed the items from each body that would make them easily identifiable, including wallets, jewelry, and car keys. After I had all of that discarded into the fireplace, minus the valuables worth keeping, I dragged the bodies into a pile at the entrance to the study. When I heard the doorbell ring, I thought it was the 'movers' coming to pack up this dead weight, and I was headed for the door until Jayson suddenly appeared again.

"Go and change your clothes because there's blood on them and meet me in the kitchen. I'll get the door," he insisted, pushing me toward the stairs.

I started to argue with him until I looked down and saw the mess I'd made of my clothing, which I knew would now have to be burned.

"Here's the payment," I said, handing him the $25K from my pocket.

"Thanks, now go."

I made my way upstairs and stripped out of my bloody clothing before selecting a maroon-colored button up and some black slacks to put on. Once I was again dressed, I went back downstairs to the kitchen and walked in to find the shock of a lifetime.

"Nice to see you again, Kwan," Tink said, smiling up at me from her seat on the bar's stool.

"H-hey, Tink. I wasn't expecting you," I replied.

"That's good because she isn't here to see you. I am," Kyndra stated.

6

KYNDRA

The look of utter shock and confusion was so cute because it was one of those rare moments of vulnerability for a nigga like Kwan. I knew that I was the last person who he expected to turn up in his kitchen, three thousand miles from the last place that he'd seen me, but the shock value was worth it.

"What's wrong, Kwan? Cat got your tongue?" I asked.

"N-nah, I'm just surprised to see you," he replied, cutting a murderous look at Jayson before his eyes came back to mine.

"Well, I figured that since I was in the neighborhood, I'd see if you survived the fire that night without a scratch on you," I said, looking him up and down.

I knew that he could hear the accusation in my tone based on the sheepish look that appeared on his face, but that wasn't enough to excuse his behavior. After what had happened between us, I felt like I deserved an explanation.

"Tink, let me show you the amazing view from

upstairs," Jayson suggested, quickly grabbing my cousin's hand and disappearing from the room.

The silence that followed their departure was instantly thick enough to choke on, but I was comfortable with it because I could tell that he was uneasy.

"So, uh, are you in New York on business or pleasure?" he asked.

"I came out here on business but seeing you this flustered has turned this into pleasure just a little bit."

"I guess that I deserve that after the way that I handled things. I'm sorry, Kyndra, and I swear that I wasn't trying to hurt you."

"So, what exactly were you trying to do? I mean, other than throw my emotions into a complete tailspin and make me wanna kill you for playing in my face?" I said, feeling the familiar warmth of anger spread throughout my body.

"Playing in your face wasn't anywhere near my intention. I was genuinely feeling you, and for once in my life, I just went with those feelings instead of questioning them and overanalyzing them. It felt good, and when we ran into each other again at the gallery, it felt like destiny or something."

"So, why did you disappear like a tiger at a Las Vegas magic show?" I asked, confused.

"Honestly because I don't believe in coincidence. The fact that a suspicious fire broke out with me and my brother in the building had me thinking that someone was trying to make a move on us. We're businessmen, true enough, but at our core, we're street niggas with enemies that got long memories. The last thing that I wanted to do was to get you caught up in what could've potentially been all-out warfare, so I vanished into the night like any good thief would," he replied, crossing the kitchen until he was standing right in front of me.

Him being this close scrambled my senses for a second, and I couldn't speak. I could only look up at him and pray that my heart wasn't in my eyes. I didn't know if what he was saying was the whole truth, but it made more sense than the wild shit that I'd been mentally entertaining over the past few days.

"How do I know that you're not lying to me?" I asked.

He didn't respond for a few moments, and then, he suddenly held out his hand for me to take.

"I can prove it. I'll trust you if you'll trust me."

I gave his proposition genuine consideration because trust was a helluva thing to ask for from anybody, let alone from a nigga that I'd just met. The fact that I'd trusted him with my body, or that I was still wearing the ring that he'd bought me, were irrelevant to what he was asking of me now. Strangely enough, it wasn't doubt that was holding me back or causing me to pause. It was the feeling I had in my gut that if I took his hand, I'd never be the same again. There was a tiny voice in my head that whispered that this was exactly what I wanted all my life, and that part scared me, but not enough to make me back away. I reached out and took his hand.

"If you break my trust, I'm gonna kill you," I vowed, looking at him so that he could see just how serious I was.

"Same goes for you, sweetheart. Now, come on."

He pulled me off of the bar stool and led me out of the kitchen, down the main hallway, until we came to a set of closed double doors. He paused before opening the doors and turned toward me.

"Last chance to walk out of the front door and forget that you ever met me," he said.

"I'm not going anywhere, Kwan, so let's get this over with."

His pause lasted a few more seconds, and then he pushed the doors open wide. The first thing that I noticed was the tasteful decoration of the study and the warmth that it gave off, and then I noticed the three dead bodies occupying space a few feet from us.

"Friends of yours?" I asked, looking at him.

"On the contrary, those are people that thought I was their friend. Now they're just memories."

"Do I even wanna know how long your memory is?" I asked, looking back at the dead people, wondering what exactly they'd done to end up here.

I wasn't about to touch them for any reason, but based on the fact that their blood was continuing to flow and pool, it was obvious that they were fresh kills.

"My memory is long, but nobody has died by my hand that was innocent."

"Well, I guess that I can respect that part of it," I said.

"You're taking this a lot more calmly than I would've expected," he said, pulling the doors back closed.

"How did you think that I'd react? With tears and hysteria? Sorry, boo, I'm not that type of bitch. Plus, it's not like this is the first time that I've seen dead people."

The look that he gave me was one of genuine curiosity, but it was the lazy smile that followed that had my pussy lips trying to eat my panties.

"Don't you *dare* look at me like that because you won't so much as smell this good pussy again if you pull another disappearing act. Understand?" I asked, poking him in the chest to emphasize my point.

He nodded his head in understanding, but that smile only got wider as he pulled me into his arms. I went with little reluctance, and before I knew it, he had my lips and mouth under a spell whispered by his tongue that was devouring pieces of my soul with his passionate kisses. With each second that passed, I felt my will to resist evaporate, and I was ready to go against the vow that I'd made to myself about not fucking him no more. The only thing that saved my pride was the sound of the doorbell ringing, which interrupted our vibe.

"I gotta get that, but I want you to wait for me in the kitchen. Please," he requested, kissing me again with a soft tenderness.

"It better not be no other bitch."

"And give you a reason to cut me or kill me? I think not," he replied, chuckling.

Despite his finding amusement in what I said, I still gave his ass a look to convey my seriousness before I headed back the way that we'd come. I could feel the smile stretching my face as I breezed back into the kitchen, but I didn't try to hide it because I felt genuine relief that Kwan had trusted me and was obviously interested in more than the casual. I didn't know exactly what that 'more' was, but I thought that it was about time for me to assert my own dominance into this situationship that we were in. I made a quick call to set things in motion and set up an appointment, sent a text to confirm my meeting later in the day, and then I made myself at home by finding something to eat. By the time Kwan walked back into the kitchen fifteen minutes later, I was flipping the last of the four pancakes I'd made while checking the sausages in the next pan.

"I see that you got comfortable," he said from behind me.

"Yep, so just know that you need to have my key made by the time I get back from my meeting this afternoon."

"I like it when you're demanding," he said seductively, placing his hands on my hips as he kissed my neck in a real gentle way.

"Don't start something that we don't have time to finish right now," I said, reluctantly stepping out of his reach and putting the food on two plates.

"Oh, we've got plenty of time. Would you like a tour of the rest of the house?"

"What I would like is for us to share a meal and talk. Now, meet me at the table," I said, smiling as I moved past him with the food in my hands.

I caught sight of his nostrils flaring, which told me that I didn't even have to look behind me to know that he was on my heels like a loyal golden retriever. I sat both plates down, grabbed the syrup from off of the counter, and then brought the orange juice from the refrigerator.

"Should we call Tink and Jayson?" he asked.

"For what? I didn't cook enough for either of them. Besides, if I know my cousin then they're somewhere naked, getting full off of each other."

"No wonder we ain't heard a peep from them, and I'm so glad that I paid extra for the soundproof walls," he replied, chuckling.

"Soundproof, huh? We'll have to test that theory sooner rather than later. For now though, we need to talk."

"Now those are the words that every man wants to hear," he said sarcastically.

"Coming from my mouth, they are because it means that I find you worthy of a conversation and maybe more. In this case, it could be so much more," I said, smiling devilishly at him.

"Mmm, I'm definitely intrigued by this salacious conversation you're promising."

I laughed out loud at the dramatics of him making his eyes get bigger as he stared me down.

"Pass the syrup first because a bitch is about two deep breaths away from being hangry," I demanded.

Once he did that and I handed it back so that he could use it, we ate in comfortable silence for a few minutes. It was his phone going off that interrupted us, but all that he did was check to see who was calling before he pressed the ignore button.

"One of your other women?" I asked calmly.

"Nah, just some business I gotta handle. I'll be out of town for a couple of days, but you're more than welcome to stay until I get back," he offered.

"Actually, I've got a little business trip of my own, so our schedules actually line up for the moment."

"What exactly is it that you do anyway?" he asked curiously.

"I'm in the antique's business that's run by my father, so I guess it's the family business. We locate rare artifacts, jewelry, paintings, etc., and once we have them, we find a buyer who's willing to pay us a generous profit in return."

"Hmm, sounds lucrative," he replied while thoughtfully chewing his pancakes.

"We do alright, probably not much more than your car dealerships."

The way that his eyebrow arched in a comical way made me laugh because I knew that his mind was already doing the math.

"If you're making money like that, then our first vacation together is on you," he insisted.

"I'll compromise with you on that. The first vacation *has* to be on you because it's tradition, but because I fuck with you, I'll let you pay for the second one too."

My logic caused him to choke on his food, which made me laugh until tears poured from my eyes, and I was forced to be merciful by pouring him a glass of orange juice.

"Y-you're trying to kill me," he stammered, still trying to regain his composure.

"Not at all, bae, not at all. I do need you to come with me though without any questions."

At first, he looked at me like I was joking, but when he didn't see a smile appear on my face, the look of curiosity reemerged on his.

"Where are we going?" he asked.

"No questions, just trust me."

I stood up from the table and offered him my hand. He paused for a moment, but then he took it and rose to his feet. Without a word, I led him from the house, outside to my car that was parked right in front.

"Hop in," I said, nodding to the passenger side of my SUV.

"Who the hell has a Lamborghini truck in crowded ass New York?"

"Obviously someone from out of town, but don't worry because I know my way around. I spent a lot of time in the five boroughs in my younger years," I replied, smiling nostalgically.

"Someday we'll have to swap stories," he said, chuckling.

Once we were both in the truck, I pulled off with the speed and reckless precision of a New York cabbie.

"If you crash this muthafucka, I'mma make you pay full price for a new one," he threatened, grabbing the armrest like it was his new best friend.

I laughed for about ten minutes straight, but he didn't think a damn thing was funny. When I finally parked the car ten minutes later, he was all too happy to get out until he realized where we were at.

"What are we doing here?" he asked, looking over the hood at me.

"I thought that you trusted me."

"I do, but…"

"No buts, Kwan. Just leave your gun in the car and come on," I said, walking around the SUV until I was at his side.

He glanced around with paranoia swimming in his eyes, but he eventually slid back inside my ride and pushed the gun under the passenger seat. A big part of me could understand his paranoia because there was little doubt that this was the same pistol that had ended the lives of the three muthafuckas he'd shown me. What I was about to do would show him that I meant him no harm though.

"What now?" he asked, climbing back out of the SUV and closing the door.

"Now I'mma show you what forever looks like."

I grabbed his hand and instantly felt the slight tremble in his fingertips, but that didn't deter me from my mission. We made our way upstairs and inside the lower Manhattan courthouse where I led us to the clerk's desk.

"May I help you?"

"Yes, I have an appointment with Justice McKenna," I replied.

"Okay. You must be Kyndra Fulher."

"I am, and this is my fiancé, Jakwan Riley. I appreciate you performing this wedding ceremony on such short notice. We just couldn't wait to get married," I said, smiling at Kwan.

7

KWAN

My first thoughts were littered with disbelief because I didn't think that there was any way that Kyndra was serious about us getting married right here right now. The look in her eyes was saying something different though.

"Let me talk to you for a second," I said, pulling her away from the justice of the peace and into a corner of the room.

"You should see the look on your face right now."

"I'm glad that you think this is a joke because it's definitely not," I said, fighting to keep my voice under control.

"You're right. It's not a joke because I'm serious. Dead serious," she replied, looking me squarely in the eyes.

There were so many things that I wanted to say, but only one question leapt from the tip of my tongue.

"Why, Kyndra?"

"Why? Do I really need to answer that?" she asked, holding up her ring finger for me to see the engagement ring that I'd bought her.

"That's not much of a reason, and you know it, so tell me what's really going on."

"What's really going on is that you asked me to trust you before you opened the doors to your study, and I did that without requiring you to do the same. Given what we shared in that moment, it's only natural to me that our bond outlive the statute of limitations, and what I refuse to do is be a liability or a loose end," she replied in a hushed tone.

I opened my mouth to argue that I could never hurt her, but I knew that my logic would fall on deaf ears because I had yet to let her into my heart. She needed to see the man that I was inside. She needed time, and that was what she was asking me for. I didn't have a good reason not to give it to her, and if I was being real with myself, I definitely wanted to get to know her in ways that I'd never known another woman. I gave her a decisive nod, took her hand, and led her back over to the justice of the peace.

"Are we ready?" Mr. McKenna asked.

"Did the marriage license get faxed over?" she asked.

"It did, so all that you two need to do is fill it out and we can get this show on the road," Mr. McKenna replied, sliding paperwork toward us with a pen for each.

I glanced at her one more time, just to make certain that she was absolutely sure about this, but I found her already bent over the desk, filling out the papers.

I followed her lead, and half an hour later, we walked out of the courthouse officially husband and wife. We made the drive back to my place in silence, but we held hands the entire way, and I could feel everything that words couldn't express.

"Hold up," she said when I moved to get out of the truck after she'd parked.

"What's wrong?"

"Nothing is wrong. I just want you to open the glove box and grab your present," she replied, smiling mischievously.

I didn't know what else to expect from her, but when I opened the glove compartment, I immediately started laughing.

"Turnabout is fair play, I guess," I said, pulling the ring box out and opening it.

"My thoughts exactly, husband."

The thick band was platinum, and the stones in it were diamonds and emeralds. When I put it on and held my hand up, she put hers next to mine, and it was clear to see that the rings were part of a set.

"You went back to the same jeweler?" I asked.

"Mmmhmm, and don't worry because the band that goes to my ring is on hold for you to go get it because I told Bethany that you'd be back eventually."

I could only laugh at her arrogance, but I pulled her toward me and kissed her passionately so that she could feel my true appreciation. When I pulled back, her eyes blazed with fire and need, glowing more green than brown in the hazel swirl of gorgeousness.

"Let's take this upstairs," I said, kissing her hand that was clenched in mine.

She nodded, and we got out of the truck. When we reached my front door, I scooped her up into my arms, causing her to laugh as I unlocked the door with my palm print while she pushed the door open.

"Remind me to add you to the security system," I said.

"Don't worry, I will, and I have to do the same with you at my places."

"Where did you two disappear to?" Tink asked, appearing in the hallway in front of us, wearing the shirt that Jayson had on the last time I'd seen him.

"I could ask you the same question, bitch," Kyndra replied as I put her on her feet and closed the door behind us.

"Wait a minute! Cuz, I *know* you didn't!" Tink squealed, jumping up and down.

"What's all the noise about?" Jayson asked, coming into the hallway from the kitchen with his shirt off, wearing only his boxers.

"These muthafuckas done snuck off and got married!" Tink said, throwing her arms around Kyndra.

"Yeah, right," Jayson said, looking at me.

When I didn't say anything, his eyes automatically went to my rung finger, and then his mouth opened wide in disbelief.

"Wooooowww! My nigga, are you serious? You really got married?" Jayson asked.

"What can I say, bruh? When you know, you know," I replied, smiling from ear to ear.

"Well, congratulations," Tink said, letting go of Kyndra and rushing into my arms.

I hugged her close like we'd known each other a life-time instead of less than a week because her genuine happiness was contagious. Jayson still wore a look of disbelief, but the way that he was looking at Tink had me thinking that they could be soon to follow in our footsteps.

"Not to sound callous, but you know that we've got that business meeting with our Midwest affiliates, so now isn't exactly the time for a honeymoon," Jayson said.

"Don't worry, my husband already told me that he has to go out of town on business for a few days, and I'm good with that because we have business of our own," Kyndra said.

"Wait, what? Can't we put that off for a few days?" Tink asked, stepping out of my arms and going back to Jayson's side.

"Bae, it's okay. Go handle your business and get that bag because I love a woman who got that same ambition that I move with," Jayson said.

"How long will you be gone?" Tink asked, pouting slightly.

"No more than two to three days," I said.

"Any more than that and I'm coming to find you myself, and shit will get ugly quick," Kyndra warned, turning to face me.

"I like it when you're feisty," I replied, pulling her into my arms.

"Come on, bae. Let's give the newlyweds some privacy so that they can at least consummate their marriage before we gotta go," Jayson said.

I was glad that the nigga had read my mind exactly because I had every intention of making Kyndra a slave to this good dick before letting her out of my sight. When I looked down into her beautiful face, I could tell that her and I weren't thinking on the same wavelength though.

"As much as I would love that, my husband, we can't consummate right now."

"Why not?" I asked quickly.

"Because we both need to clean our respective houses. I'm not naïve, Kwan, so I know that you were fucking somebody before you just so happened to bump and grind into me. And I ain't been a virgin in a long time. Now, I know that I can't kick no pussy out of your past, just like you can't kick no dick out of mine, but we can make our start fresh by cleaning up our past. That's the best way to prevent shit from getting messy later on because I know firsthand that a bitch somewhere is willing to act a whole muthafuckin fool bout that good dick you got. Don't make me kill someone for no reason," she said seriously.

"Makes sense," Tink said.

"Does it really?" Jayson asked, looking at Tink with caution.

"Actually... it does," I replied, already picturing the one female in my mind that I needed to sit down with.

When I leaned down to kiss Kyndra again, my lips held the promises that I intended to keep once we met up again.

"Don't forget that I know how good that pussy is too, so don't get a nigga's whole family killed," I warned, looking down into her mesmerizing eyes.

"I hear you, baby, and you ain't got nothing to worry about because I've been stingy for years now."

After dropping another quick kiss on her lips, I turned her loose, even though I really didn't want to. It still blew my mind that we'd actually married each other, but for reasons beyond my ability to explain, it felt right, and I wasn't afraid to embrace that feeling.

"Tink, get dressed because we gotta go," Kyndra said.

"Jayson, follow her lead," I added.

While they went to do that, I took my wife by the hand and led her back to the study.

"Kwan, I really don't need to see the dead people again. I get it; you're dangerous."

"That's not what we're doing, smartass," I said, chuckling while pushing the doors open wide and leading her to my desk.

"I know that I didn't imagine those three dead people in a heap a little while ago, so where did they go? And who cleaned up that mess?" she asked, looking around, slightly bewildered.

"None of that is important, sweetheart, but I promise to tell you all of my secrets when we have a few years to talk. For now, I just wanna make sure that we can communicate privately."

I reached into the bottom drawer of my desk and pulled out what appeared to be a normal iPhone, which I turned and handed to her.

"Place your finger on the screen so that I can recognize you as the owner and operator," I instructed.

Once she did that, the screen lit up, and the word 'loading' popped up, only to vanish a few seconds later.

"My other iPhone doesn't do that."

"This one does because it's encrypted. We can talk about whatever we want on there, including through text messages, and it would take NASA the better part of ten years to crack the encryption," I said.

She looked up at me with an expression that carried hints of suspicion.

"Do I even want to know why a supposedly legit businessman would need something so clandestine?"

"First of all, I am a legit businessman, but my clientele are some of the richest one percenters in the world, and I can't always vouch for their business practices. Secondly, in this day and age, it's always best to assume that 'big brother' is watching because a healthy dose of paranoia is better than the alternative," I replied.

Her eyes stayed locked on mine, and I could see her processing my words for the proper context to put them in. I could tell that she was skeptical at the very least, but based on her non pulsed reaction to me killing three people, I doubted that she had any illusions about who I really was. All that remained to be seen was whether or not she could accept it.

"There's obviously a longer conversation that we need to have, but it can wait. Program your number in here for me," she said, extending her new phone toward me.

I pulled my phone from my pocket, unlocked it, and then tapped it against hers so that my contact information was instantly transferred.

"I'm ready, cuz," Tink called from the doorway.

"Be safe," Kyndra said softly, taking a step forward and pulling me toward her for one last kiss.

The instant electricity from her mouth jump started my desire to put her on my desk and run it back for the night that we didn't get to finish what she started at the gallery. I would've indulged too and said fuck work, but she backed away before I could draw her in all the way.

"To be continued," I said with a wicked smile.

"Promises, promises, my husband."

I watched her juicy ass and thick thighs saunter away

from me like I was hypnotized, and I was still seeing those visions long after I heard the front door close.

"Married though, my nigga?" Jayson asked, appearing in the doorway and leaning against the door's jam.

"Yeah, I know that it's crazy."

"Nah, it ain't crazy; it's muthafuckin suicidal! How are you gonna explain this to Rashawna?" he asked, chuckling softly.

As soon as he said that name, I felt a cold chill race up my spine, and the vision of a beautiful face popped into my mind. The history between Rashawna and I was something that would make a really good book someday, but I might not be alive to write it if she killed my ass for getting married.

"I can handle Rashawna."

"Sure you can, but just make sure that you leave your will and life insurance policy in a place where they can be easily found," he replied, laughing.

I gave him my middle finger to laugh at before I returned to my desk and turned my computer on.

"So, what's your plan, Romeo?" he asked.

"I'd rather do the notification over the phone, but something tells me that she's only gonna want to kill me if I'm a coward about it. So, I guess I've gotta go see her," I replied, booking my flight from D.C. to Kentucky for tomorrow night.

"What do you want us to do?"

"I'm gonna drive to D.C. and then fly to Louisville. You and the team head out there today and begin the recon that's necessary, and we'll go operational once I join you," I replied.

"Make sure that you have your bulletproof vest on and tell Rashawna I said what's up," he replied, still laughing as he walked away.

I wanted to dismiss what he was predicting her response to be as an exaggeration, but I knew Rashawna, and I'd seen her crazy come out. This knowledge was a good enough reason to take the coward's way out and just text her an update on my marital status, but I respected her too much for that. I ran upstairs to pack a quick overnight bag and swap my dirty gun out for a clean one before heading outside to flag down a taxi.

I took a cab to our car dealership in uptown Manhattan where I selected a convertible, sky-blue Bugatti off the showroom floor. Within ten minutes, I was on the road, speeding into the unknown while trying to prepare an adequate break up speech for a woman that I'd been fucking for the last nine years. I made the six-hour drive in just under four and a half and texted Rashawna to meet me at her townhouse in Georgetown once I was inside the city limits. Her response surprised me because she said that she was already home, and that was different because to my recollection, she never took any days off. I pulled up at her house fifteen minutes later, and after debating with myself for a few minutes, I decided that it was in my best interest to keep my gun on me going in. By the time I made it up her front steps, she was pulling the front door open, and I got two eyes full of her naked body.

"We're fucking first; we can talk later," she stated, pulling me inside by my shirt.

There was no time for me to argue.

8

KYNDRA

New Jersey

"Sorry that I'm late, Daddy. Something came up at the last minute," I said, walking into the kitchen with a new spring in my step.

"It definitely did," Tink added, following in my footsteps and chuckling softly.

I started to turn around and smack the shit out of her, but the stern look on my father's face was my focus now.

"You seem to be in great spirits for someone who missed the score of a lifetime," he said with evident disdain in his voice.

I felt my anger rising, but I knew that he was just trying to bait me, so I kept a straight face.

"Well, Dad, word on the street is that there's a $100 million dollar bounty on whoever robbed the gallery, so I'm glad not to have that price tag on my head. You should be glad too because, undoubtedly, they would've killed you to get to me," I said, taking a seat across the table from him and taking a piece of toast from the pile on the plate between us.

"She's right, Uncle Kenny. It would've been a sweet lick, but nobody lives to spend that kind of money with that type of heat on their head," Tink added, joining us at the kitchen table.

"Being scared ain't part of this game, and obviously someone was willing to take the risk because the robbery happened, and the mastermind is still in the wind. In case those details escaped either of you," he replied snidely.

I had some smart shit to say, but I kept it to myself because it wasn't worth the argument in the end.

"Did you call me down here for a lecture on your perception of my ineptitude?" I asked, biting the toast and chewing it slowly.

"Yes and no. Contrary to my perception of your ineptitude, I still enjoy seeing my beautiful daughter and niece in person and not just on a video screen."

"Aww, that's sweet, Uncle Kenny," Tink said, smiling.

"Just wait, there's more," I said dryly, knowing my father all too well.

I'd had years to study this man before me, and although I was his only daughter and favorite child, I still knew this man like I knew myself. Right now, I knew that something was wrong. For a few moments, he just stared at me, and I returned the favor in between chewing pieces of toast slowly and waiting for the other shoe to drop.

"First things first, there's an interesting job out in Texas, but it's a little different than usual," he began.

"Different how?" I asked cautiously.

"Because the value isn't in money or jewels; it's in a person."

"Hold up. You want us to kidnap a muthafucka?" Tink asked, looking back-and-forth between me and my father.

"That's the job," he replied nonchalantly.

"Who's the person?" I asked, curious despite the distaste in my mouth at the idea.

"It's just a truck driver's daughter, and it's a simple catch and release job."

"Then, I don't get it. What are we snatching her for?" Tink asked before I could.

"Because her father drives for one of the cartels, and this run includes enough fentanyl to supply the entire West Coast for a month," he replied.

My mind immediately started running numbers, and it didn't take me long to realize that we were talking about at least a metric ton or more of weight.

"There's no way that all that dope is in one truck," I said.

"Glad to see that you're still quick on your feet, sweetheart. And you're right. It's not in one truck; it's in a three-truck caravan that's escorted by a helicopter watching from the clouds," he stated.

"Oh, great. That sounds like an easy target to hit," I said sarcastically.

"You don't gotta worry about the helicopter, but you're gonna need three drivers to take over the trucks in order for you to get away," he replied.

"What about the trucks' GPS?" Tink asked.

"Whoever is monitoring that won't see anything out of the ordinary because you'll follow the same highway route to the next rest stop where more trucks will be waiting for you to transfer the dope," he said.

"This is sounding less and less like an 'us' job and more and more like a 'we' job," I said, looking at my father closely.

"Sweetheart, you already know that if you need my resources then you're more than welcome to them."

He was saying all of the right things, but if this shit was as smooth as he said it was, then he probably could've pulled it off without my help or involvement. I didn't know what it was, but there was definitely something that he wasn't telling us.

"What's our window?" I asked.

"The shipment leaves Mexico tomorrow night, and based on the spot I picked for you to make your move, you should be on them by sunrise."

"What about the girl?" Tink asked.

"You all need to snatch her as soon as possible because she's the only guarantee you have that the driver will go along with your plans. If you take a flight to Dallas tonight, then you should have plenty of time to scoop her up before she goes to school in the morning. Her mom's dead, so she's literally all he has left."

The coldness and calculation of my father's tone was something that I'd grown accustomed to, but that was a long way from me liking it. As far back as I could remember, he'd been telling me not to take shit personal because this world ran smoother when you saw shit as nothing more than business. Destroying a family was purely business to him, but the sadder part was that I understood and shared his philosophy because I'd lived it for years.

"Why wait until tonight to fly to Dallas? Why not go now?" Tink asked logically.

"Because you've gotta go clean up your mess first," he replied, looking squarely at me.

I had no idea what he was talking about, but I had no doubts that this was the shoe I'd been waiting for to fall from the sky.

"What mess?" I asked neutrally.

"It would seem that a certain NFL quarterback didn't keep that amnesia that you gave him because I'm hearing whispers about him trying to void the sale of his real estate company. From what I've heard, he has a judge in D.C. who's a friend and has a lot of pull, so that issue requires your immediate attention."

"What's her name?" Tink asked, pulling her phone out.

"Rashawna Goode," he replied.

The next sound I heard was Tink's fingers flying across her phone's screen, and a few minutes later, she turned it toward me so that I could see the picture of an attractive brown skin woman. I pulled out the phone Kwan had given me, unlocked it, and tapped it against Tink's phone to transfer the information from her quick search. I immediately sent it to Skylar and told her to hop the next flight to D.C. so that this slight inconvenience could be taken care of. Even though I knew that my phone was completely secure, I couldn't say the same about Skylar's, so I kept my explanation to a minimum. All she really needed to know was that the judge had outlived her expiration/sell-buy date, and it was a definite greenlight to release all of the edited footage on the all-American quarterback.

"It's being dealt with. Tink, book us two seats on the

next flight to Dallas," I said, looking up to meet my father's steady gaze.

"You're not getting sloppy or lazy on me, are you, Kyndra?" he asked softly.

My father wasn't the biggest man in the world, but it was something about his 5'10", one hundred eighty-five pounds that was imposing when he seemed quiet and reserved. There were only two times in my life that I'd seen my father lose his temper, but even then, it had been a quiet fury that resulted in four different men forfeiting their rights to continue breathing. That was the reason I wasn't afraid of Kwan, but my father was as intimidating now as he was when I was ten years old.

"Of course not, Dad. You know like I do that the only way to control a mark is to kill them, but that wasn't the original plan because I thought that he had too much to lose for him to call my bluff. Like I said though, it's being dealt with," I stated unflinchingly.

He continued to stare at me in silence for a few more moments before he finally nodded his head.

"Our flight leaves in an hour and twenty minutes, so we need to go," Tink said.

I dropped the remainder of my toast on the plate, stood up, and came around the table to kiss my dad on the forehead.

"I love you, Daddy."

"I love you too, sweetheart. Oh, and don't think that I didn't notice that beautiful engagement ring weighing your finger down. That's a conversation for later though."

"It's just a ring, Dad," I said, giving him my best innocent look.

"Yeah, uh huh, just make sure that you let the nigga know that he's gotta come to see me sooner than later. It's better if he does it voluntarily so that I don't gotta send for him."

Tink's sudden laughter earned her a death stare, but I didn't say what I was thinking.

"I'll see you later, old man," I said, hugging him and then heading for the door.

"Bye, Uncle Kenny," Tink said, following behind me.

Neither of us spoke until we were in the car driving away.

"Well, that went better than expected, all things considered," Tink said.

"That's easy for you to say when he's not demanding to meet your nigga."

"Come on, Kyndra, you knew that he was gonna peep that big ass rock on your finger and do the math. Your dad ain't never been a slow one."

"No, but he's obsessively possessive and has scared more than one nigga off before," I reminded her.

"True, but we both know that Kwan ain't no type of bitch nigga who's scary."

Her statement caused my thoughts to do an immediate shift to my husband, and I felt myself smiling as my body heated up like he was touching me in the gallery all over again.

"Damn, bitch, at least *try* to hide some of your fucking teeth!" Tink said, laughing.

I laughed with her, not ashamed of the hold that this virtual stranger had over me.

"I want you to keep that same muthafuckin energy when it comes to Jayson, bitch."

She stopped laughing immediately, and I could see her staring at me out of the corner of my eye.

"That's different," she replied in a serious tone.

All I could do was laugh harder and shake my head because it was obvious that the dick had my girl gone already. A big part of me wanted to tease her mercilessly because Tink wasn't the type to fall for just any nigga and definitely not one she'd just met, but our minds needed to be focused on business.

"We can revisit this conversation after you're married to Jayson, but for now, let's put our mind on the tasks at hand," I said.

"Okay. I'm assuming that you already got Skylar handling the quarterback/judge situation, which means that we've got Dallas in our sights. Who do I need to contact in that part of the country to assist us because we're definitely gonna need some hittas?"

I gave this question careful consideration because I didn't want a bunch of hittas that would shoot first and ask questions never. This wasn't a mission to run the body count up because a certain amount of finesse was needed to successfully jack metric tons of cartel dope. It was also gonna take some niggas with nuts the size of monster truck tires because the consequences for crossing the cartel was something that would surely be televised.

"What do you think about bringing Psyco and his niggas out to play?" I asked, glancing at her as I merged onto the causeway that would take us to the airport.

"Are you talking about D.C. Psyco or Psyco from Little Rock, Arkansas?"

"Little Rock," I replied.

"Shit, them niggas is *big* crazy, and they give no fucks, but them Eight Trey Gangsta Crip niggas have proven loyal so far... It could work," she said, nodding as she went about typing a message on her phone.

Within ten minutes, Psyco had hit back, only too eager to come up on the million dollar payday that we were offering. We'd done business with him before, but part of me was still apprehensive because the amount of dope that we were lifting was likely to be more than any of them niggas had seen in one place.

"Listen, we use them for the initial hijacking, but we don't need them for the switch because they might be too tempted to pull a triple cross," I said.

"You took the words right out of my mouth."

"I mean, I know Psyco fucks with us, but this is life changing money we're talking about," I said.

"Are you wondering why Uncle Kenny put us on to it?"

"I'd be lying if I said that I wasn't trying to figure out his angle, but so far, it's not clear. In time, he'll reveal his hand though because this shit is too big for him to hide the truth indefinitely," I replied with confidence.

"Have you thought about what you're gonna tell Kwan and when?"

This question had been dancing in the back of my mind ever since I'd fortuitously ran into him in the jewelry shop in L.A., but I still didn't know how to break it to him that I was a born and bred criminal. I couldn't say for sure when his acceptance began to matter to me, whether it was after we fucked or after he showed me those dead bodies, but it mattered. It wasn't that I thought that he'd judge me or not understand. It was just that I liked the squeaky-clean image that he had of me. It had been a long time since I'd been that girl.

"I ain't really got that far, Tink. I mean, we were married for like ten minutes before we had to go on separate business trips. After we make it through this, I'll figure it out."

"We'll figure it out because I wanna be real with Jayson too," she said, smiling shyly.

"Aww, that's so cute!" I said, teasing her.

"Fuck you, bitch!"

We both laughed, and I could tell that she felt as giddy as I did about the prospect of sharing a life with someone. We all had money and material things, but this life never really left room for anything that looked like love. Somehow, we'd both found successful Black men who could handle the strong Black women that we were, and that felt good. We spent the rest of the ride daydreaming out loud about double dates, having a lavish joint destination wedding ceremony, and one day raising our kids together. By the time we boarded our flight, it was like we were both walking on air, and neither of us wanted to come down. It wasn't until hours later when the pilot announced our imminent landing that we put our newfound happiness aside and screwed our game faces on. It was time to get back to running that bag up because there was plenty of time for happily ever after later on.

9

KWAN

Washington, D.C.

Her lips were as incredibly soft as I remembered, and she still knew how to kiss with enough passion and skill to make any coherent thought in your mind take a long vacation. For a few seconds, I gave into her blindly, but then I finally mustered enough strength to unlock our lips for a moment. I had the perfect excuse on the tip of my tongue, but it was impossible to deliver while I was looking down into her chocolate-colored eyes that were made even more sexy by the obvious Asian heritage that was simmering somewhere within, giving them an exotic shape. The rest of her 5'10", one hundred thirty pounds was even more undeniably beautiful, and I couldn't stop my eyes from wandering downward in order to fully drink in her nakedness. I could hear my breathing change as my heart hit my chest cavity at a quicker rhythm, and I could feel the pheromones she was giving off working their magic.

"I missed you, Kwan... Didn't you miss me?" she asked in a tone that sold sex without any effort.

I opened my mouth to offer some type of response, but she didn't let a word get out before her mouth was back on mine, delivering CPR lessons. I was so wrapped up in her kiss that I didn't feel her hands working my zipper until my dick was outside of my pants, aiming at her like a .762 round. She wasted no time dropping to her knees and opening her mouth wide in acceptance. The torturous part was that she just waited patiently, mouth open, while she looked up at me in a blatant challenge for me to use her submissive will at my own risk.

The good guy in me fought valiantly against the temptation for about 1.5 seconds, and then, my demons came out, forcing me to take the small step forward required to push my dick past her succulent lips. Instantly, her lips locked around the head like a wall socket accepting an extension cord, and she left little doubt as to who had the power. She sucked me slow at first, making sure to take my dick deep down her throat so that I felt the heat and snug fit that always drove me insane. After a couple minutes of that, I could feel my dick beating like a bass drum, and I felt like I could knock two of her teeth out if she wasn't careful. I felt like Trey Songz because I didn't wanna leave the warmth of her mouth, but I had to go right the fuck now! When I pulled back out of her mouth, she immediately hopped to her feet and then jumped into my arms while wrapping her legs around my torso.

My instincts took over, and without conscious thought, I pushed my still throbbing dick up inside of her as I carried her through the house. The first room that we came to was the half bathroom on the ground floor, and I immediately entered and put her on the sink. The grip of her legs increased in strength as she braced for what she knew was coming, but by my third stroke, she had to relax because my dick was hitting her too deep. My rhythm wasn't too fast; it carried just enough speed to give her long strokes that she couldn't recover from. She tried to lift her hips and fuck me back, but when my hand went to her delicate, slender neck and I pushed her back until she was in a reclined position against the mirror, all she could do was take the pressure of my pounding. When her pussy's grip fought back, I fucked her hard enough to bruise her walls and deliver more pleasure. When it felt like a dam burst within her and she cried out, I fucked her faster until passion torched us both within its flames, and I came hard enough to make me weak at the knees.

"T-taking the day off w-was such a great move," she panted, smiling at me.

The guilt that I instantly felt was a completely new and foreign feeling to me. I needed a moment to process it internally before I spoke, so I just put my dick away and backed up.

"What's wrong?" she asked, wiping the sweat from her brow and climbing down off of the sink.

"Nothing."

"Jakwan, when did we start lying to each other? I've known you for a while, not to mention that I'm a judge, so I'm trained to know bullshit when I hear it," she said, standing in front of me with a less than patient look on her face.

"It's nothing, I've just got a lot on my mind right now."

"And sex ain't helping? Well, damn. I know that I ain't losing no steps, so you must be going through some serious shit. Does this have anything to do with it?" she asked, grabbing my left hand and holding it up between us so that my wedding ring was visible.

It took all of my strength and experience to keep my face set in a neutral expression, but I managed to pull it off.

"Nah, that ain't it," I replied, pulling my hand away from her.

"Oh. So, this must have something to do with the genius robbery that took place on the West Coast," she said, walking out of the bathroom.

Rashawna and I didn't keep secrets from each other, like she pointed out. She knew exactly who I was and what I was into, even though she didn't always approve of what I did. I followed behind her because I'd detected a hint of displeasure that had briefly contorted her features before she'd left the bathroom. When I walked in the kitchen, she was standing there with the refrigerator door open, drinking from a bottle of water.

"What do you know about the robbery?" I asked.

"That's not what made you pop up unexpectedly, so why don't we start with that topic of discussion? Is that ring real, as in you're actually married?"

"That's a complicated answer," I replied slowly, trying to gauge her temperature.

"It's really not though. Either you got a wife or you don't."

"I mean, yeah, but it wasn't planned. It kinda just... happened," I said, not sure how else to explain it.

"Congratulations. By the way, I'm pregnant," she said, smiling brightly.

"Wait, hold up, you're *what*?!" I asked in shock and disbelief.

"Pregnant, Kwan. You know, with child, expecting, as in I'm gonna have a baby."

"But-but I thought we..."

"Relax, my nigga. It ain't yours. I just didn't want there to be any questions later on," she said, finishing her bottle of water and tossing it into the trash.

I suddenly had a lot of questions bombarding my brain because the last time that I'd checked, her pussy belonged to me and only me. Obviously, I was all the way wrong. I chose not to focus on that though because she wasn't playing twenty questions with me about my sudden marriage.

"Now that we got that out of the way, what do you know about the robbery?" I asked again.

"Just that it was smoothly done, and it smelled like something that you would be into. I have a feeling that you didn't make any new friends though because you made off with some seriously valuable shit. Allegedly."

"Having enemies ain't new to me, and I've got no fucks to give. I'm just curious as to what's being said behind closed doors," I replied.

"Well, from what I heard, only a nigga with a death wish would've tried to make a play on that particular exhibit, which was kinda what told me that it was you and your crew."

I let her words wash over me without taking offense to the obvious insinuation about me not valuing my life. It wasn't a death wish that motivated my decisions. It was just that I didn't give a fuck because I felt like anybody could get it in this world. I'd always feel like that until somebody proved different to me.

"So, did you fuck me because you wanted one last ride just in case someone actually manages to punch my ticket?" I asked with a smirk.

"Not at all. You happened to show up right when I needed you because my sneaky link had to cancel our lunch date, so I figured that you could feed me dick and then food. Let me go throw some clothes on."

The smile that lit up her face was as infuriating as it was gorgeous, and all I could do was chuckle as I shook my head. When she left the room, I went to the kitchen cabinet where I knew she kept her good liquor, and I pulled out a bottle of scotch along with a glass. I poured two fingers and tossed it down my throat, tasting nothing but heat, and then I poured the same amount in my glass again before returning the bottle. With my drink in my hand, I took a seat at her kitchen table and sipped it before I sent a quick text to Jayson, letting him know that I was still alive. It took him less than a minute to send back three laughing crying emojis, which I could only shake my head at.

"Damn, does the wife got you day drinking already?" she asked, breezing back into the kitchen wearing a white, off the shoulder dress and some low top, white Jordan IVs.

She'd piled her hair up on her head in a messy bun, and the freshly fucked glow on her skin only enhanced the still undetectable pregnancy. For a second, my brain scrambled, and I started thinking with my dick, but I shook that shit off as I downed the rest of my drink and stood up.

"Rashawna, if you wanna ask me about my wife then do that but keep it cute."

"Touché, touché," she said, raising her hands like I'd pulled my gun on her.

"Whatever. Where are we going to eat?"

"It's a surprise, so give me your keys," she demanded, holding her hand out expectantly.

I only hesitated for a moment, and then my curiosity got the best of me, and I dug in my pocket to give her what she wanted. She gave me a quick, unexpected kiss on the lips in return and then led the way outside. Once we were in the car, she had us speeding through traffic, heading farther into northwest D.C., and twenty minutes later, we arrived at a new Jamaican restaurant.

"I ain't never ate here before. Is the food any good?" I asked.

"Of course it is. I only hired the best cooks from Jamaica and flew them out here."

"Wait, you own this spot?" I asked, looking at her somewhat shocked.

"Did you think that the name on the building was a coincidence, Kwan?"

Up until that point, I hadn't even looked at the name. I'd just known what type of food it was because I was familiar with the smells of authentic Jamaican cuisine. Her statement caused me to pay attention now though, and I chuckled softly.

"A friend of Shawna? That's cute," I said.

"I'm glad that you think so because I spent some of your money to get it just the way that I like it," she said, getting out of the car.

I followed her lead, but I didn't chastise her about spending the money because she knew that I would've given it to her had she asked anyway. I didn't simply invest in things; I invested in people because the return was always better. When we got into the restaurant, she surprised me by waiting in line for seating like any typical customer would, and we were seated within five minutes.

"I like to monitor how the restaurant really runs by popping in like this and getting the genuine feel like the average person," she explained once we were seated with our menus.

"That's actually a sound business practice. Why don't you order for both of us?"

"I think that I can do that," she said, motioning for a waitress to come over.

While she ordered our food and drinks, I pulled out my phone and booked my seat on the next flight to Louisville International. Changing flights from my later time cost a little more, but it didn't matter because I'd done what I'd set out to do here.

"You know better than to think that you're gonna have your face in your phone with my sexy ass sitting across from you. Don't play with me," she said seriously.

"Relax, Mama Bear. I'm just taking care of my flight out."

"Flight? Where are you headed to so soon?" she asked, pouting sexily.

"I've got some business to handle, and it can't be put off."

"Okay, so then why exactly did you grace me with your

presence for the whole five minutes that you've been in town?" she asked, beginning to sound and look annoyed.

I knew from several firsthand experiences how hot her temper could get, but I also knew that the lady in her wouldn't let her act a damn fool in public. Even though she was only twenty-seven years old and one of the youngest judges on the federal circuit ever, she had years of maturity that women twice her age hadn't mastered. This was a better opportunity than I'd hoped for to keep shit a buck with her.

"I came out of respect to tell you to your face that I was married," I replied.

Her initial response was to look at me with major skepticism, but then her features softened gradually.

"That doesn't sound anything like the Jakwan that I know. You're not a nigga who needs closure."

"Maybe not, but I am a nigga that respects your heart," I said genuinely.

Her mouth opened, but she quickly shut it, and I realized that she didn't know how to respond. This was the first time I could ever remember her being speechless, and it was cute as fuck.

"I'm sorry, Kwan."

"Sorry? For what?" I asked, confused.

"The baby. I mean, I didn't plan on getting pregnant by anybody right now, but sometimes life just be life'ing. And I don't believe in abortion, so..."

"Rashawna, I would never even *suggest* that you do no shit like that. I know that we didn't put any titles on us or say that we were exclusive, but that doesn't change the love that I have for you. Or the fact that I'll be a part of your child's life no matter what. You don't owe me any apologies. I just want you to be happy, and I hope you know that I'm always here if you or the baby need anything," I said sincerely.

The smile that lit up her face and the sexy way that she bit her bottom lip had my brain fighting for control because my dick was trying to jump back in the driver's seat. Thankfully, the waitress reappeared with our drinks, and a waiter pulled up with her, carrying our food. With the tough conversations now out in front of us, we were able to just kick it like old friends and lovers, and before I knew it, a whole two hours had passed.

"I'mma miss my flight fucking with you and this delicious ass food. Can you drop me off at the airport?"

"What about your car?" she asked.

"Consider it a baby gift. Hopefully you give birth to a baby boy."

"If I do give birth to a hardheaded ass little boy then I'm naming him after you, and he's gonna show up on your door like a package from Amazon Prime. Go ahead and let your wife know now," she replied, standing up.

I laughed even though I knew that she was serious, and I followed her lead out of the restaurant back to the car.

"Next time that you come to town, bring me that new Maybach truck," she said, giving me her most seductive smile.

I was just about to spit out a smart-ass retort when a speeding black Jeep Cherokee caught my attention. One second, it was a few feet away, and the next, it was right on top of us with a mean looking Draco hanging out of the window attached to a gloved hand.

"Rashawna!" I yelled, reaching for the gun at the small of my back.

As soon as my hand found my gun's grip, I knew that it was too late because she was already turning toward the sound of screeching tires. Bullets flew fast, and I saw her body take direct hits before she collapsed to the blood-soaked pavement. By this time, my gun was out, up, and barking killer intentions at the fast-fleeing Jeep, but I knew it wasn't enough. I knew that I was too late.

10

KYNDRA

Thirty-six Hours Later

"I just got word that the trucks are about fifteen minutes away from us," Skylar said.

I nodded while looking out the window from my seat in the back of the navy-blue Chevy Suburban. My eyes were trained on the direction that they would be coming from. We were currently sitting at the truck stop where the robbery would take place, and everything had been set in motion for this thing to run like clockwork. The little girl on the seat beside me was still asleep from the heavy sedative, so she was blissfully unaware that she was in the middle of a potential warzone. Psyco had seven cars full of his homies spread out around the truck stop. This seemed like too many niggas to bring out for a job this simple, but his logic of being prepared wasn't something that I was gonna argue with. Contact with the driver had been made, and the rules had been set, but the other two drivers were cartel and that made them the definite wild cards. My instructions to Psyco had been to simply shoot them and anything that looked like them.

"Tink, let our drivers know to be ready because they need to be in those trucks and back on the road in under two minutes," I said.

"I got you," she replied from the front seat.

Her voice sounded distracted despite the fact that her phone was in her hand, and I knew that there was currently only one nigga that could take her mind off of the money.

"Tink, I love you, but if this move gets fucked up or we die because you're distracted by Jayson, please know that I'm gonna kill you over and over like a horror movie," I warned.

She gave me a sheepish smile over her shoulder, which confirmed her guilt, and then she got out of the car and walked two cars over to where our drivers sat waiting in a green F350 pickup truck.

"Why would her mind be on ole boy from L.A.?" Skylar asked, turning around in the driver's seat to stare at me.

"It's a long story."

"It sounds more like a kept secret, bitch, now spill," she insisted.

At first, I didn't say anything. I just tried to stare her down into submission so that she would let the topic go, but after a few moments, I had to accept it as a lost cause.

"When we went to Jersey to visit my dad, we kinda made a detour into New York first so that she could see about the Rolls Royce truck that she wanted," I replied.

"Uh huh... and?"

"And she saw Jayson," I replied nonchalantly, averting my gaze to look out the window again.

"Who did you see?"

Her question made my eyes snap back to hers as I felt the heat of a flush on my face, and my mind suddenly filled with images of the man that was impossible to forget.

"The drivers are ready," Tink said, sliding back into the passenger seat.

"Good. Let's keep our minds sharp and focus on the business at hand," I replied, giving Skylar a pointed look.

She chuckled as she turned back around in her seat, but she let the topic go for now. It wasn't like I trusted Skylar any less than I did Tink, but there was a part of me that didn't want her to feel like the third wheel. I knew first-hand that Skylar didn't have any problem whatsoever getting a man or woman, but I knew that she'd see the situation with me and Tink as double dating. I didn't need any type of discord or dick to come in between me and my crew. When I pulled my phone out, my intentions were to simply let the compromised truck driver know to leave the truck running and that he would find his daughter sleep on the backseat of the stolen SUV. The plan went sideways though because I couldn't take my own advice, and after texting the driver, I found myself texting Kwan for no other reason except for the fact that I missed him. What made it worse was that I could feel myself literally holding my breath waiting on him to reply, and I had to force myself to breathe.

"Bitch, why are you back there breathing like Baby D off of *Next Friday*?" Skylar asked, looking at me in the rearview mirror.

Tink glanced back with a concerned look on her face, but as soon as our eyes locked, she burst into laughter.

"Fuck you, bitch," I said, shaking my head in disgust with myself for being so transparent.

"I wish you two hoes would let me in on the inside joke," Skylar said, sounding annoyed.

"The joke is that this bitch is a hypocrite because I'd bet my share of this heist that she's back there texting that nigga, Jakwan, right now," Tink replied, still chuckling.

Before I could utter a word in my own defense, a text message hit my phone, and it had my undivided attention because, in my heart, I knew that it was from Kwan. As soon as I read his words, my blood turned to ice, causing my whole heart to freeze.

"Oh, God," I murmured, feeling suddenly nauseous.

"What is it?" Tink asked, getting real serious real quick.

"It's-it's Kwan. H-he said that somebody tried to shoot him in broad daylight," I replied, already texting back as fast as my shaking fingers could manage, needing more info.

"Is he okay? Was Jayson with him?" Tink asked quickly.

"He didn't get hit, but somebody did because his first message said that he was leaving the hospital," I replied.

I didn't even have to look up and see Tink's face because I could feel her fear.

"Well, Jayson ain't in the hospital because I was just texting him, but I'll see what he knows," Tink said.

"All that is gonna have to wait. The trucks are here," Skylar said.

When I looked up, I saw three identical black and white

eighteen wheelers slow creeping into the truck stop, and there were four black SUVs trailing them. As badly as I wanted to put my entire being and focus onto Kwan and what he was dealing with, I knew that I couldn't afford that. I had to handle the business. I immediately texted Psyco and told him to hit the SUVs as soon as I gave the signal. Once the trucks came to a collective stop, one driver climbed out of the cab and headed in our direction.

"Let's do this," I said, putting my phone in my pocket and pulling my black Glock .42 out.

Our exit from the SUV was so casual, as to appear nonchalant to passersby, but high alert was all that we knew in moments like this.

"Wh-where's my daughter?" a slender built, white man asked, approaching rapidly.

I couldn't explain why I did what I felt happening, but my pistol was suddenly levelled at his face, and I squeezed off two shots without speaking a word.

"What the fuck?" Skylar asked, spinning around toward me with disbelief on her face.

I ignored her and turned my attention toward the two tractor trailers that were still occupied.

"Get the other drivers," I said, motioning with my gun in hand.

The echo of gunshots brought the whole parking lot alive within seconds between the cartel's blockers in their SUVs and Psyco's people. Flames were flying like we'd brought the entire circus to town, and my gun was a contributing factor as I took aim at the cab of the tractor trailers. Once I was sure that the drivers weren't gonna be a problem for us anymore, I turned toward the F350 and motioned my drivers into position. Despite the heavy fire-fight, they got out, and each man zigzagged his way to a truck. Within moments, the trucks were pulling out of the truck stop as fast as they could, and I knew that our mission was halfway complete.

"Let's go!" I yelled, motioning Skylar and Tink back to the SUV we'd come in.

"Kyndra, what the fuck was that?" Skylar asked as she threw the truck in gear and chased after the eighteen wheelers.

"That was me leaving one less witness and doing this little girl back here a favor. You know like I do that the cartel was gonna kill her father anyway for losing their load, and they more than likely would've killed her first just to make it more painful for him. So, I spared her life by taking his."

I knew that both women probably wanted to argue with me, but it would be a losing battle because my logic was sound. Plus, I'd never admit that I made the split-second decision while running off of the emotional high from what happened to Kwan. I couldn't let them know that my husband had me off of my game in any way. Everything inside me wanted to pull my phone back out, just to see if he'd texted back yet, but I didn't wanna carry that guilt for someone dying as a result of my inability to lead them when it counted the most. It wasn't just a battle that I was having with myself; it was an all-out inner war going on. When I caught sight of the trucks through the windshield of the SUV, I felt a new surge of adrenaline because the job was almost complete, and then I could focus on Kwan.

"Catch up to them," I demanded.

A few seconds later, we were riding their bumper, and we stayed there for the twenty minutes it took for us to arrive at the next truck stop. The security cameras that monitored this lot had already been disabled like the ones at the last truck stop, thanks to Skylar, so we had the necessary time to make the switch.

"Sky, disable the GPS on all the trucks and trailers. Tink, tell our drivers to drop the trailers, switch cabs, and then get back on the road."

"Which route do you want them to take?" Tink asked.

"Tell them to head northeast toward Montana because that's our destination," I replied.

"Why Montana?" Skylar asked.

"It's a good spot to lay low where no one except for us knows what we're doing there. Plus, being way out there will give me time to figure out what my father is up to," I replied.

Tink hopped out of the SUV, and I saw Skylar grab her laptop before I heard the sweet music that her hacker fingers could make. For the moment, everything was under control, and I couldn't find one good reason not to pull my phone out and have a quick peek. When I did, I was relieved to see that I had a message waiting from Kwan, and when I read it, I was able to breathe slightly easier. In my heart, I knew that I couldn't achieve deep breath status until we were in each other's arms again, but knowing that he'd escaped unscathed did my heart some justice. There was no logic behind my attachment to this man, even though we were married on paper, but I didn't care in the slightest. I could be logical everywhere else in my life, but I'd always wanted that crazy type of love that no one understood except for that person in it with me. When I sent him a message, asking him what his plans were, he told me that he still had business to handle, and then he planned on putting all of his resources into finding the muthafucka who'd taken a shot at him. I told him to keep me posted, and I was now able to refocus on what I had going on. It took another fifteen minutes for the cab swap to be finished, and once we'd gassed up, we were back on the road right behind them.

"How are we unloading the trucks once we get to Montana?" Tink asked.

"We'll figure it out if it becomes necessary, but for now, we can just park them on the one hundred thirty acres we acquired from the quarterback," I replied.

"Speaking of him. After I took care of his judge friend, I released all of the video footage that you complied that night —_after I made sure to blur out our faces," Skylar informed me.

"Thank *God*! The last thing that I need is to try and explain that shit to Jayson," Tink said.

"Ain't no way that nigga thinks you're a virgin, cuz," I said, laughing.

"Fuck you, bitch! He know I ain't no virgin because I rode that dick good and proper, but I don't need him thinking that I'm no damn ho neither. Niggas don't be trying to turn hoes into housewives no more."

"Housewife? Bitch, you know that you ain't ready to get married to no nigga, regardless of how good the dick is," Skylar said, laughing.

When she realized that Tink wasn't laughing with her,

she cut her eyes in her direction, and then her expression changed.

"Wait, are you really thinking about getting married? To a nigga you *just* met?" Skylar asked.

"It don't matter how long you know somebody because when you know, you just know," Tink replied defensively.

"Kyndra, talk some sense into your crazy ass cousin before this dude have her ass sold into a sex trafficking ring or something, or she wakes up in the Sudan missing a kidney."

I knew damn well that I had no room to criticize Tink, especially given the fact that I was already married, but this wasn't how I'd wanted Skylar to find out.

"It's her life, and if she feels like Jayson is the one, then we've gotta respect that and support her decision," I said.

"Okay, who the fuck are you two doppelgangers and what have you done with my bitches who would fuck em and leave em before they *ever* thought about marriage?" Skylar asked.

"We still the same, so shut up," Tink replied.

"Nah, it's something different about both of you, and I can smell it on you, so spill," Skylar insisted, looking directly at me in the rearview mirror.

I kept steady eye contact with her until I caught Tink turning to face me out of my peripheral vision. I only had to glance at Tink to know what she was thinking, and I knew that there was no way to make it all the way to Montana and keep my marriage a secret.

"I got married yesterday," I confessed, looking back at Skylar through the rearview mirror.

At first, she didn't say anything, and then, she started laughing.

"Yeah, right, Kyn. I might believe some crazy impulsive shit like that coming from Tink, but I *know* how close you and your independence are."

"If I hadn't been there after it happened, I wouldn't believe that shit neither, but I saw her when they got back from the courthouse, and her face was glowing like she was pregnant," Tink stated.

I wanted to tell her to shut the fuck up because she wasn't helping, but I kept my mouth shut to give Skylar time to process it. It was a full ten minutes before she spoke again though.

"Kyndra, I love you, but I hope that you know what you're doing because it's not just your life that you're putting at risk with your decisions."

"I understand that, and I promise that no harm will come to anyone because of my decision to marry Kwan," I vowed.

"I'm gonna hold you to that," Skylar replied.

I knew that she meant what she said, but I didn't feel the need to convince her beyond what I'd already said. Instead, I put my focus back on the trip in front of us. It took us six hours to get to the mansion that Michael Newcome used to own, and once we were there, everyone was ready to fall flat from exhaustion. I got the drivers set up inside the ten room estate while Skylar and Tink picked their own rooms, but instead of following their lead, I went back outside to check the inventory. In the back of the first truck, I found wall to wall compressed bricks of white powder that I assumed was fentanyl. I expected to find the same in the other two trucks, but the surprise that awaited me forced me to call Skylar and Tink back outside.

"We've got a problem," I said immediately after they arrived.

"What is it?" Tink asked.

"My dad lied. Two of the trucks don't have dope in them," I replied.

"What was in them?" Skylar asked.

"Gold and platinum bars and each truck is full of them."

11

KWAN

Atlanta
Two Days Later

"What's up, bruh? What's on your mind?" Jayson asked, walking up behind me and standing at the balcony railing by my side.

I'd lost track of how long I'd been standing in the same spot, looking out at the beauty of the nighttime Atlanta skyline, while not really seeing anything because my mind was hundreds of miles away. A big part of me wanted to be by Rashawna's hospital bed as she fought for her life, but until I knew which one of my enemies had taken a shot at me, I couldn't risk putting her in any more danger with my presence. Guilt was such a foreign feeling to me that I felt like I was literally choking right now, and I didn't know how to fight it. I just had the insatiable urge to kill someone.

"I'm just thinking about Rashawna," I said softly.

"How's she doing?"

"When I spoke to her father earlier, he said that she was stable, but-but they couldn't save her baby," I said, feeling the bile rise in the back of my throat.

Jayson wasn't the one to offer up hollow platitudes, so he gave his support by passing me the blunt that he'd just lit. As a rule, I only smoked during down time, so I took the weed readily and filled my lungs with the potent smoke until my mind was swimming in an infinity pool. The problems didn't go away, but at least the sound of the guilt screaming at me was put on mute for a moment.

"Any word on who made a move against me?" I asked.

"No, and at first, I thought that Fabian wasn't looking in the right place or asking the right questions."

"Except that we know firsthand just how thorough Fabian is," I said, passing him the blunt.

"Exactly, so that got us to thinking outside the box, and we moved beyond the assumption that you were the target. Rashawna may be a respected judge, but she's a judge nonetheless, and they're always bound to have enemies."

My instinctive response was to dismiss this theory, but the weed allowed my mind to be open to the impossible, and suddenly, I saw myself playing the shooting back in mental replay. I'd made the natural leap into thinking that I'd been the target the whole time, and Rashawna had simply been hit because she'd been on the side of the car closest to the street. Now that I was really thinking about it though, I had to admit that the trajectory of the shots didn't fit that theory. I was a big enough target to be seen and hit over top of the car, but not one bullet had come anywhere near hitting me.

"Who would wanna shoot her?" I wondered aloud.

"That's the same question that I posed to Fabian, and he's still digging so that he can compile a complete list of all of her known enemies. One thing that he found already sounds interesting though. So, you know those tapes that were released about the Washington Commanders quarterback and his lifestyle of fucking whores and using drugs? Well, he knew Rashawna, and he talked to her a day before the shooting according to her phone records. Since those tapes came out, he's been saying that he was hacked and blackmailed and that he was actually robbed by the women in the video. No one was buying that shit, except that you know there have been whispers in our circles about a female crew that is with the shit. What if the whispers are true?" he asked, passing me the blunt back.

"So, you're saying what? That they're trying to kill Rashawna for trying to help the quarterback?"

"I'm saying what would we do in that type of situation?" he countered, looking at me knowingly.

I didn't give a quick response, choosing instead to contemplate and smoke some more.

"So, who are these women?" I asked, passing him the rest of the blunt.

"And therein lies the mystery, bruh, because nobody knows. Whoever they are, them bitches are brilliant because they don't leave a trail for anyone to follow, and they don't bother with petty jobs. Word on the street is that they're crazy enough to rob the Mexican cartel, and you know like I do what type of job that is."

"Suicidal," I said, suddenly more intrigued.

"Exactly. And I'm not saying that they're behind what

actually happened to Rashawna, but you were there. Were the shots meant for you or for her?"

"Honestly, I'm not sure anymore, bruh. I mean, I ain't no little nigga, and the only thing standing between me and Rashawna was the Bugatti coupé we came in. By that logic, I should've at least got hit once or grazed," I replied.

"Do you remember anything about the shooting other than what you already told us?"

I started to shake my head when a brief glimpse of the driver of the Jeep popped into the forefront of my mind.

"The-the driver. I didn't remember it until just this instant, but the person behind the wheel was a white girl with red hair. She could've had a wig on, but she was definitely a white female behind the wheel," I replied.

"Okay, I know that Fabian is still working backwards through the traffic cams, but he still ain't found a way to restore the wiped footage from the day and time of the shooting. He's hoping to get lucky and catch a glimpse of the person or persons canvassing the restaurant since Rashawna owns it and obviously spends time there. He said that whoever hacked the traffic camera wasn't a rookie, and you know that was a begrudging compliment."

"Tell him to keep looking but let's not ignore the obvious because we did make the enemy of the Chinese triad. We need to consider the possibility that our involvement was leaked before I could silence our partners," I said.

"Yeah, we're already working that angle too because they're the most obvious suspect. Did Rashawna tell you who the baby's father was?"

"No, why?" I asked, looking at him closely.

"Because we can't ignore the fact that she might've

gotten pregnant by someone who didn't want her to have the baby or someone who already had a family and couldn't risk exposure."

My initial quick response was to deny the possibility, but I had to keep my mouth shut and admit that I really didn't know who she'd been fucking. I'd thought that I'd been the only one until she'd told me differently.

"I'll find out who the nigga was," I vowed, knowing that the questions would be easier coming from me.

The sound of my phone ringing interrupted us, and I pulled it from my pocket to answer it.

"Hello?"

"Hey, handsome, do you miss me yet?" Kyndra asked.

The sound of her voice immediately lifted a weight off of my shoulders, and I felt myself smiling for the first time today.

"Based on the look on your face, I know who that is," Jayson said, chuckling as he walked away shaking his head.

I ignored him and focused on my wife.

"Of course I miss you, sweetheart, just like I know that you're missing me," I replied.

"Has anyone ever told you that your arrogance is sexy?"

I laughed out loud because my arrogance had been called a lot of things, but sexy wasn't a word used to describe it ever.

"You're just saying that because you're my wife."

"Oh, nah, I'm definitely saying it because it's true," she insisted, laughing softly.

"Okay, I believe you. So, what's up? When will I get to see you again because it's been too long already?"

"Well, that's actually why I'm calling because I was thinking the same thing. Where are you?" she asked.

"Atlanta. Where are you?"

"Headed to Atlanta. I can be there in a few hours," she replied.

"I've got a better idea. Why don't you clear your schedule for the next week and let me give you the honeymoon that you deserve?" I suggested persuasively.

"Sounds mysterious and I like it. Where are we going?"

"I'll let that be a surprise. Just tell me where you are right now so that I can arrange for your travel from the nearest airport," I replied.

"Okay, hold on, bae."

While she had me on hold, I thought about all the different places that I could take her, trying to decide what best fit the bill for the privacy and seclusion that I wanted. Nothing about our relationship had been normal or typical, but it was a priority to me that I got to know her better. Rashawna getting shot served as a reminder of how short life could be and how the unexpected could appear at any time to fuck up the harmony of your plans. I didn't wanna miss out on a moment with Kyndra.

"Baby, the nearest airport is in Butte, Montana," she said.

"Montana? They got Black people in Montana?"

My question caused her to laugh, but I was serious.

"Of course they do. Now, are you gonna tell me where you're taking me?" she asked, sounding more than a little excited.

"Nope. Just get your sexy self to the airport, and I'll meet you in a different time zone."

"Yes, Daddy," she replied seductively.

I laughed as I hung up and immediately used my phone to make her travel arrangements. The private jet would pick her up and fly her to me in Atlanta where it would do a quick refuel before we took off for one of my favorite places in the world. Once the travel plan was complete, I contacted my housekeeping staff at our destination and alerted them of our imminent arrival so that they could get the house ready. I was just finishing that up when Jayson poked his head back out onto the balcony and motioned for me to come inside. For a brief moment, the strong feelings of disappointment washed over me because I felt like whatever he was about to tell me would fuck with the plans I'd just made. But I made the conscious decision not to let that happen. When I walked back inside, Jayson was waiting for me, but he didn't say nothing. He just led the way into the living room where Blaze and Fabian were seated in front of the TV.

"What's going on?" I asked.

"Michael Newcome was just found dead in his mansion in Maryland," Fabian replied.

"Suicide?" I asked, not surprised.

"Nah, it was murder. His wife shot him point blank in the face with a ten gauge shotgun," Blaze replied.

"Damn," I mumbled, vividly imagining the mess that someone had to clean up after that.

"That's not why I called you in here though," Jayson said, passing me his phone.

When I looked down at it, I saw a naked image frozen, but when he tapped the play button, the body started moving, and the show became clear.

"Is there a reason that you got me watching porn right now?" I asked, looking at him in confusion.

"The faces are blurred out except for Michael Newcome's, and not even Fabian can hack through whatever is blocking them. I can't be one hundred percent sure, but I think that's Tink," Jayson said.

My eyes shifted back to the phone as my finger tapped the replay button, and I watched again with this new possibility in mind.

"There's no identifying marks or tattoos, so what are you basing your assumption on?" I asked, looking back toward Jayson.

"I know how she fucks."

We both knew that this was a hollow argument at best, but I didn't wanna dismiss him out of hand like I somehow had more intimate knowledge of the chick that he was fucking.

"Okay, so if you're right then what does this mean?" I asked.

"Look at the chick in the threesome with her," he replied.

Again, I hit the replay, only this time, I watched the white girl instead of the Black one, but this brought me back to a state of confusion in the end.

"What am I missing because, right now, all I'm seeing is a white girl that I'd test drive around the block my damn self," I said, admiring her technique.

"You said that the driver of the Jeep was a white girl with red hair, right?"

"Jayson, ain't no way you made that leap from this video," I said dismissively.

"Why not? If she was one of the people that set ole boy up, and he went to Rashawna for help, then why wouldn't she be a part of the cleanup crew?" he asked logically.

"Well, first of all, you know like I do that there's a big difference between a robbery and a homicide. But let's say that this woman had the killer instinct all along, then why didn't she kill the quarterback from the jump? Why give him the opportunity to be a liability? And let us not forget that the women Michael Newcome was known for fucking were high dollar hoes."

"Those are all valid points, bruh. Except being the driver ain't the same as being the shooter, and that's something that we all know too. And letting the quarterback become a liability is the gamble that anyone takes when you get greedy and go for the robbery *and* the extortion. As for Mr. Newcome's choice of companions, shit, that would only make it easier to get to him if they posed as high dollar hoes," Jayson replied.

"Okay, so what are you saying? You think that Tink and this white girl are part of a two-woman crew?" I asked.

"Nah... I think that it might be deeper than that," Jayson replied.

"Meaning what?" I asked, feeling impatient.

"That answer would require asking the most obvious question... Who's the person filming the whole thing?" Fabian asked.

For a second, my mind went blank, and then the implication hit me between the eyes like a fast-moving bullet seeking to destroy my place of peace.

"So, you think that my wife is involved?" I asked, looking around the room at each man.

No one responded, but in truth, that was answer enough.

"You niggas can't be serious. So, what's next? You all are gonna tell me that me running into her in L.A. was part of some elaborate plan on her part?" I asked, feeling my anger mount swiftly.

"Are you not willing to admit even the slightest possibility in all of this?" Blaze asked.

"Sure, but it's a farfetched possibility at best, my nigga. Need I remind you all that we were in L.A. on business, and my decision to go to the jewelry store was spontaneous. There was no way for Kyndra to arrange that meeting."

No one said anything, and that frustrated me as much as the crazy shit that they were trying to get me to entertain.

"I'll tell you what. Why don't you all focus on keeping us off of the triad's radar, and I'll worry about Rashawna and Kyndra," I said, passing Jayson his phone back before I headed for the door.

"Where are you going?" Jayson asked.

I didn't even bother to respond. I just kept on walking to the elevator and took it down to the lobby. Once I was outside, I had the valet bring my silver Maserati around, and then I raced off into the night. There were a few errands that I needed to take care of before I headed to the airport, so that was where I put my focus and energy. By the time I had finished up with that business, the need for a nice relaxing vacation was all that I had eyes for, and I got to the airport just as the G-V touched down. When I boarded the plane, I went straight to the cockpit to give the pilot instructions about his final destination, and then I headed to the back where I expected to find Kyndra fast asleep. When I opened the door, I found her hazel eyes sparkling mischievously as she laid on the bed naked with a smile on her face.

"Come show me how much you missed me, Kwan."

12

KYNDRA

It was something about catching him off guard that always made my pussy wet, but it wasn't until now that I figured out why. Kwan was calculating, almost ruthlessly so, but from all appearances, I made him just as unsettled in a good way as he did me. That was extremely rare, and in this case, it worked like an aphrodisiac.

"What are you waiting for?" I asked, slowly spreading my legs.

I watched his eyes widen slightly as they traced the soft flesh of my inner thigh, up to my pretty pussy that was secretly aching for him. The sounds of the jet's engines roaring to life promoted him to shut the door and start shedding his clothing like a kid about to hop in the deep blue waters of his dreams. He kneeled on the king-sized bed, and before he even touched me, I felt my skin turn feverish. I didn't know what to expect, so when he started kissing and licking his way up my inner thighs, I had to work hard to contain my excitement. He kissed my pussy lips with all the patience of a skilled lover trying to convey a message to which I was only too eager to receive because my legs continued to spread like the button on my garage door opener had been pushed. When his lips wrapped around my clit, it started to throb instantly, sending a signal through my entire body that brought each single nerve ending to life. His suction was gentle, patient even, but when he lashed out at my clit with his tongue, my back arched like a McDonald's sign. He used his right hand to gently push me back to the mattress, but his mouth was still showing very little mercy. My legs locked around his neck of their own accord, and I thought that he would've tried to fight against them, but he proved that he wasn't claustrophobic by diving deeper into my pussy. The way that he focused on my clit felt like someone gave him the cheat code to my anatomy because even when he slipped his tongue into the deep waters between my pussy lips, he always returned to the faucet that made the water run. He devoured me until I came hard enough to force my eyes shut while I screamed loud enough to drown out the jet's engines. At first, I thought that I was hallucinating when the plane started to roll, but then it registered to me that we were headed for takeoff.

"B-baby, the plane," I panted.

"Shhh," he whispered, kissing his way up my body until he got to my lips.

The taste of my pussy on his breath was new to me, but I fell in love with it and kissed him with renewed intensity as I felt his dick slowly push through the gateway to my walls. Our first sexual encounter had lacked this gentleness, but now that he was giving it to me like this, I swore that I could feel him in my soul. He fed me every inch like an artist with an eye for detail, only to pull all the way out of me and do it all over again. With each stroke, the popping sound of my pussy reluctantly releasing the vice grip I was putting on his dick got louder and louder until it overpowered the jet throttling up.

By the time the plane tilted toward the sky, my world was doing the same thing, and Kwan was all I had to hang on to. I felt my nails pierce the taunt flesh of his back, but that only succeeded in causing his muscles to flex as he fucked me harder. Before the plane leveled off, I lost the fight to his dick, and I came all over it with delirious pleasure. If he thought that would tire me out though, I knew just how to surprise him and turn the tables. I swiftly rolled him onto his back without letting him escape my walls, and then, I was in control. The pressure of his throbbing dick told me what speed to set, and before he knew what hit him, I was riding him at a full gallop. Every time I slid back up his shaft until only the head of him was trapped inside me, I swiveled my hips like a hula hoop champion. It took me three minutes to drain all of the cum out of him, and only then did I allow myself to collapse on his chest from exhaustion and accomplished satisfaction. The way that his arms automatically went around me and pulled me close damn near felt better than my orgasm, and I felt myself smiling into his chest. It wasn't my intention to nod off, but the next thing that I knew, the vibration from the plane bouncing off of the runway brought me back to consciousness. The fact that I was still on top of him, his dick was still very much inside me, and he had obviously been comatose as well took away any embarrassment that I might've felt.

"Mmm, good morning," I said.

He stretched like a well-fed lion and smiled up at me.

"You damn right it is."

"So, are you gonna tell me where we are since you fucked me into a coma, and I couldn't get any info from the pilot beforehand?" I said, sitting straight up and rocking back-and-forth ever so gently.

"It's-it's just a spot that's my sanctuary."

"Oh... really?" I asked, rocking just a little faster as his dick got harder inside me.

"B-baby, wait. Let's take this to the villa," he said, grabbing my hips and holding me in place.

I could feel my own defiance due to my body's demand for sexual fulfillment, but the promise of what was to come gave me the strength that I needed to climb off of him.

"You owe me."

"And I promise to pay you in full," he replied, sitting up in bed.

We both quickly got dressed, and by the time that the plane stopped rolling, we were ready to go. When the door opened, I stood there in shock, looking around like I'd just landed on another planet because we were definitely on another continent. I hadn't paid attention to the word play when Kwan had suggested that we take our sexual exploits to the 'villa' instead of the house, but as I looked off into the distance, I could see the difference.

"Where are we?" I asked, amazed and excited.

"It's a little spot called Santorini."

"It's absolutely beautiful," I said, walking down the stairs to the tarmac.

There was a navy-blue Ferrari awaiting us, but there were two men in customs' uniforms standing between us and the ride.

"Welcome to Greece, Mr. and Mrs. Riley. May we see your passports please?"

"I uh…"

"They're right here," Kwan said, reaching over my shoulder and saving me from trying to make up some lame excuse.

I held my breath as the two men huddled together to inspect the documents because I knew that there was no way in hell Kwan had given them my real passport. That was tucked away in a safe that he knew nothing about. All I could do was hope that whoever he got to do the forgery had done quality work because I was too cute to go to jail in a foreign country.

"Very good, sir. Enjoy your stay," one man said while returning the passports to Kwan.

After that, they stepped aside and allowed us to get into the waiting sports car.

"Remind me to ask you later how the hell you pulled that off," I said, chuckling and shaking my head.

"It's a secret… but I'll tell you mine if you tell me yours," he replied cryptically.

"It's a deal."

He studied my face for a few seconds, almost like he was looking for some hidden truths, but he didn't say anything to illuminate his thoughts in this moment. Instead, he started the car, and we pulled off.

"So, where are we going?" I asked.

"Well, first, I'm gonna feed you, and then we're gonna go shopping for some essentials. After that, I'll show you around my safe place."

"Sounds like a plan but you better be careful because I could get used to being treated like a pampered queen," I warned, smiling at him.

"As you should, sweetheart. You deserve the royal treatment, and it's my privilege to bring your princess dreams to fruition as the queen that you are."

The feeling of his praise washing over me was comparable to nothing I'd felt before, and I never wanted that feeling to fade. With any other nigga, I probably would've worried about that happening sooner than later, but Kwan was a different kind of man altogether. His stamina extended beyond the bedroom, and his attention to detail would make any woman feel special, so I definitely felt blessed. That feeling combined with the beauty of Greece passing outside my window had a huge grin on my face, and my expression didn't wavier in the slightest as I pulled my ringing phone out of my pocket.

"Bitch, guess where I am?!" I said excitedly.

"We might have a problem," Tink replied.

I felt my smile slip before I could consciously remind myself to keep it in place for the sake of my husband.

"What's going on, cuz?"

"I don't know, but Jayson is acting weird and asking weird questions," she replied.

"Okay... I need more details than that."

"He's talking about the quarterback that got killed by his wife, and he asked me if I'd ever met him," she said.

"Well, that don't seem like nothing too crazy, Tink."

"It is if the nigga saw the sex tape that we leaked. My face might be blurred out, but the nigga is bound to recognize my body and the movement of it," she replied, sounding more than a little panicked.

My mind flashed back to the night we laid in wait for the late Michael Newcome to surrender to his baser instincts, but I wasn't looking at it retrospectively to remember Tink's actions. I was selfishly thinking about myself and worried about the man next to me discovering my duplicitous lifestyle before I had the chance to tell him.

"Kyndra? Did you hear me?"

"Yeah, cuz, I heard, but I think everything is gonna be fine. Just keep shit cute," I advised, hoping that she was understanding that I was telling her to keep her mouth shut.

I heard her take a deep breath, and I could feel her anxiety traveling thousands of miles.

"I don't know how to spin this nigga, cuz. He's so different from other niggas that I've dealt with."

"Yeah, I know exactly what you mean," I replied, feeling my husband's energy swirl around me.

Kwan made me feel safer than I could ever remember any other man making me feel, but I knew that the flip side of that was a danger that I had no interest in provoking.

"Maybe I should just make up some excuse to put some distance between me and him," she said.

"Nah, that's not a good look on you at all. Just stick with what you been doing and be yourself. Okay?"

"Okay, cuz, you know that I trust your opinion. I'll call you if I need you," she replied.

"If I don't answer, it's because I'm getting my back

beat in, and don't blow my shit up because I'm *not* getting off the dick til I'm done," I said, disconnecting from the sound of her laughter in my ear. The fact that Kwan was laughing too made me nudge him in warning. "FYI, I wish you *would* answer your phone while I got the pressure of this good pussy on you!"

"Sweetheart, you ain't *neva* gotta worry bout no shit like that. Is everything okay with Tink though?" he asked.

"Yeah, she's just going through some girl shit. We're cousins but more like sisters for real."

"I never asked you, but do you have any siblings? Are both of your parents still alive?"

"Well, you know that my dad is alive, but I honestly have no idea where my mom is. I have two older brothers, but both of them are doing Fed time for making an armored truck disappear," I replied honestly.

"Made an armored truck... Wait, are you talking about the robbery out in Delaware like twelve years ago?" he asked, looking over at me.

"You actually keep track of shit like that?"

"I mean, no, not really, but you gotta admit that the way they made that muthafuckin Brink's truck vanish in broad daylight was genius," he replied, chuckling.

"Yeah, except for the part where they both got life sentences because the drivers disappeared too, and it was assumed that my brothers killed them in order to keep the location of the money hidden."

Kwan didn't say anything, and it wasn't until he reached out and took my hand in his that I realized how quickly tension had taken over my body due to anger. I wasn't angry with the man beside me though. I was still pissed at my father for teaching all of his children the tricks of the trade. There were a lot of times in my life that I envisioned being someone else, but none more so than when I thought about my brothers. None of us had been given a chance at a normal life, but it was too late to be bitter about it now because I was a grown ass woman who made her own decisions.

"I'm sorry, bae. I know that you're just trying to get to know me in this very unorthodox relationship of ours. I didn't mean to bite your head off," I said, squeezing his hand in mine.

"Sweetheart, we all have things in our past, secrets, that we're sensitive to talking about or thinking about. You don't have anything to be sorry for."

"Thank you for being so understanding," I replied.

He looked at me and smiled, causing my heart to melt with the same speed that my panties got soaked, and I just wanted to devour him on the spot.

"How far away from the villa are we?" I asked.

His laughter was instantaneous, and I knew that he'd read my mind just based on the question that I'd asked.

"One appetite at a time, bae. Let me feed you first," he said, pulling the car over in front of a quaint little café.

"Okay, but just know that the longer you make me wait, the more I'm gonna torture you."

"Do you promise?" he asked in a low, seductive tone of voice.

I took his hand, pulled it under my shirt, and laid it flat across my left tittie.

"Cross my heart and hope to die."

I could tell by the look in his eyes that he was tempted

to say fuck breakfast right about now too, but he kept his lust in check. That shit made me want to fuck him even more though. Instead, I followed him into the café where we enjoyed a delicious Mediterranean breakfast, and he told me about how he'd first discovered the beauty of Santorini, Greece. After we finished eating, we went on a mini shopping spree since we'd traveled this far without luggage, and then we finally headed to his villa. We passed a few different villas on our way up the winding road, but they all paled in comparison to the majestic palace he had tucked into the side of a grass covered mountain. It was two stories of exquisite brick and clay with columns that looked hand carved in the shape of a lion's head strategically placed to separate the levels.

"It's amazing," I said in awe.

"It's your wedding present. It was the one thing that I cherished the most before you, and now you're all that I'll need in this world. Don't ever forget that, Kyndra."

13

KWAN

One Week Later

The smell of crêpes and sausage made me open my eyes even though they weren't the things that had awakened me. I'd been trying to ignore the insistent ringing of my phone since it had snatched my peaceful slumber away, but after ten minutes, it was still going. In frustration, I finally grabbed it off of my nightstand.

"What, Jayson?" I asked, not even needing to look at the phone's display to know who was calling.

"You're being summoned."

"Summoned? By who?" I asked, thinking that he was joking.

"By Rashawna."

Those two words caused me to sit straight up in bed as surprise took ahold of disbelief and morphed them into gratefulness.

"She's-she's awake?" I asked.

"She woke up about an hour ago, and the first question out of her mouth was your whereabouts. How soon can you get here?"

This question made me look out the window at the beautiful bright day I'd anticipated spending with my wife, showing her the rest of Greece.

"Uh, I can't just hop in the car, bruh. I'm in Santorini," I confessed.

"Damn, nigga. I know that you said you'd be out of town, but did you really feel like going to Greece was the best move?" he asked, clearly frustrated.

"It wasn't a bad idea considering how much work we'd been putting in lately, and not to mention that someone was shooting in my general direction, if not directly at me."

"Okay, point taken, but now it's time to come home and deal with this. I'm sure that Rashawna can give us some more insight, but me questioning her ain't something that you would like or that she would go for," he pointed out.

The truth in his words and assessment of the situation were obvious to me, but I still didn't know how I was gonna explain all of this to Kyndra. I'd told her that a friend of mine had gotten hit by the shots that I'd assumed were meant for me, but that was as far as I'd elaborated. Yeah, she'd told me to clean my house, which was why I'd gone to see Rashawna in the first place, but the part where we spun the block one more time sexually was where my explanation fell apart. Kyndra and I may not have known all of each other's secrets, but I could feel her crazy in her energy, so I wasn't about to play with mine or Rashawna's lives.

"I'll be there as soon as I can. Just tell her that I'm on

my way, and I'm coming back from out of the country," I said, hanging up before he could protest being the messenger.

As I was swinging my legs out of bed and down to the floor, I was already calling to have the jet fueled and ready for imminent departure. When that was done, I threw on a white Polo shirt and some khaki Black Billionaire shorts and went in search of my soon to be pissed off wife.

"Something smells amazing," I said, walking up behind her and kissing her gently on the neck.

"Nothing too major. I just figured that I'd cook you a little breakfast since you've been spoiling me with your culinary skills all week."

"I plan to spoil you in a lot of ways for the rest of our lives," I said, turning her around to face me. She looped her arms around my neck and stood on her tippy toes to kiss me softly.

"Do you promise me because I don't want you to start something that you can't finish?"

"Oh, I can definitely finish what I start," I replied, leaning in and kissing her more thoroughly.

I was all prepared to let us get carried away in this moment, but she stopped me by putting both hands on my chest and pushing lightly.

"Would you care to explain why you just woke up and you're already fully dressed? By the way, I heard your phone ringing."

The expectant look on her face told me that I better not lie right now. The smile that I gave her in return was sheepish, but I knew that beating around the bush was no longer the option to take.

"Jayson called me to tell me that my friend who got shot is awake now."

"Ah, and she's looking for you, which now explains the persistence when it came to his phone calls," she said, nodding in understanding.

"Who said that it was a female?" I asked, eyeing her closely.

"Just a logical deduction considering that the last thing that I told you to do was get your affairs in order. Literally."

"You're right, and I did. She knows about you," I said, content to tell the lie by omitting the rest of that eventful afternoon.

"That's good, so she won't be shocked when we show up at her hospital bedside together."

Before I had a chance to list all of the reasons that was an extremely bad idea, she'd turned the stove off and was heading toward the bedroom to undoubtedly cover her beautiful nakedness with clothes. My brain scrambled in search of some more than plausible reasoning for her not to go to the hospital with me to see Rashawna, but each excuse sounded like a man with a guilty conscience. While my mind tried to work through the problem like it was college level calculus, I was able to keep my hands busy by putting the food she'd cooked onto two plates. I never got the chance to sit down and eat though because she came back into the room with her phone in her hand and a stricken look on her face.

"What's wrong?" I asked immediately.

"My-my dad wants to see me. Now."

"Okay... I get the feeling by the way that you say that

that this isn't a good summons. What's going on, baby?" I asked, moving toward her.

"I... he sent me to-to handle a business meeting, but he lied to me about what the business was about, so I didn't report back to him."

"Well, what did you do?" I asked, confused.

"I left the country with my husband and went on our honeymoon," she replied, looking at me with her heart in her eyes.

"As you should have. Do you need me to explain that to him?"

"No, that will only piss him off more. I just-I've gotta go see him and deal with it," she said, sounding defeated already.

I pulled her close to me and hugged her while resting my chin on the top of her head.

"I'm going with you," I stated, making sure my tone indicated how nonnegotiable this decision was.

"Kwan, I know that ain't no part of you bitch but going to see my dad when he's already pissed off is gonna end bad for everyone."

"I hear you, bae, and I appreciate the warning, but I'm not about to allow you to face anyone, including your father, without me by your side. We're in this together, so let's go handle business and then get back to our honey-moon," I said.

When she pulled back and looked up at me, I could see the growing love that neither of us had put into words yet, and it made me smile down at her.

"How soon can you arrange for us to leave?" she asked.

"The plane is being fueled now, so all that we need to do is get to the airport."

"Let's go then," she replied, taking my hand in hers.

In the short time that I'd known Kyndra, I'd never seen her rattled or nervous, not when faced with the death that I'd inflicted or even when we'd gotten married. I could feel the trembling caused by nerves in her fingers now though, and it made me wonder about the dynamic between her and her father. I knew that I was getting ready to step into a grey area, and most likely cross a boundary, but the real nigga in me couldn't abide by my wife being afraid of anyone except God. I made small talk with her on the drive to the airport while my mind was trying to decide the best way to handle the situations that awaited us back in the States. By the time we were on the plane taxiing for take-off, I was comfortable with my decision to go with Kyndra to meet her dad before I dealt with Rashawna. I made sure that the pilot knew that we were headed for La Guardia airport in New York, and then I called to make sure that one of my cars would be waiting. With the details taken care of, I poured both of us a generous amount of Tennessee whiskey on the rocks before taking my seat across from Kyndra.

"So, tell me about your dad."

"What do you mean?" she asked carefully.

"I mean, what kind of man is he? I need to know what I'm about to walk into."

She didn't respond for a few moments, but the way that she drained her glass was more telling than words.

I couldn't tell if the deep breaths that she took after-wards were a result of the potent amber liquor attacking her vocal cords or just her trying to steady her nerves. Either way, I was content to wait.

"My dad is old school by every definition of the word, but none more so than the fact that he expects his word to be respected like the laws of a federal statue. I remember when I was younger and one or both of my brothers would disobey or piss him off in general, and he would make them put boxing gloves on. Then, he'd beat them until they were barely conscious," she said, staring out the plane's window into the clouds.

The hollow tone of her voice did its best to hide her pain and fear, but those were emotions that I was so familiar with that I could catch their scent like a single blood drop in the ocean. Just this story alone told me exactly the type of man that her father was, and now I knew how to approach the situation.

"Where are you supposed to meet him?" I asked.

"At his place in east Manhattan."

"So, that was the business meeting that you and Tink had to go to after we got married?" I asked.

"Yeah, but I had to go to his house out in Jersey then. He's in New York on some type of business, and he's insisted that I meet him there."

"Give me the address," I said, pulling my phone out.

She pulled out her phone and recited an address that I typed into my GPS. It sounded familiar once she was saying it, but once it popped up, a few of the missing pieces started to fall into place. So did a few more questions.

"You and your brothers don't have the same last name, do you?"

"How-how did you know that?" she asked, looking at me quizzically.

"I should've done the math when you told me what they'd gone to prison for, but I was only interested in dropping that subject because of how it made you feel. The address that you just gave me is registered to Hatchet Job Incorporated, and I know that is owned by Kenneth 'Big Hands' Hatchet, former Golden Gloves champ. He's your father?"

"Yeah, but how do you know him?" she asked, clearly agitated and flustered.

Several lies popped into my head that could've been delivered with plausible believability if this had been anyone but his daughter sitting across from me. I had no doubt that she knew her father as a businessman, but it was also a better bet that she knew that he was too crooked to be straight. I didn't want her to view me the same way, but that seemed unavoidable at this point.

"I didn't even know that Big Hands had a daughter," I said, shaking my head in disbelief.

"Well, he does; I'm her, and now it's your turn to explain how the hell you know my father at all."

"Aside from being an avid boxing fan... I've done business with him on occasion," I admitted.

"What kind of business?"

"The kind that you don't put on your tax returns," I replied, giving her a knowing look.

When she nodded her head, I saw understanding in her eyes, not judgement, and I felt a little relief to go along with my building curiosity.

"What type of work do you do for your father?" I asked.

"I already told you that I help him run the family business..."

Everything inside me wanted to press the issue, but her fear was palpable enough to fuck with the jet's cabin pressure, and I didn't want her to feel cornered. So, I let the subject drop for the moment as I got up to fix her another drink. When I handed it to her, she gulped half of it down without taking a breath, but based on the trembling in her hands, it wasn't enough to calm her nerves. The protector in me hated to see that, so my mind was already trying to formulate a plan. I sat back down across from her and then motioned for her to come sit in my lap. She hesitated for only a second before draining her glass and then climbing into my lap like a sleepy toddler. I wrapped my arms around her tightly and held her until she finally went to sleep like that, but my mind was still moving a mile a minute. Once I was finally able to decide on a course of acceptable action, I was able to drift off to sleep myself. I didn't open my eyes again until we were landing, and I found Kyndra still in my lap, staring at me.

"How long have you been awake?" I asked, smiling.

"Probably about an hour or so."

"And you didn't move?" I asked, surprised.

"No. You make me feel safe, and I wanted that feeling to last for as long as possible," she replied softly.

"Baby, you're *always* safe. I understand that he's your pops, but I swore before God to protect you, and I gotta stand on bidness."

She nodded her head in understanding, but I could still

feel her fear, and it was feeding my slow building anger that had been manifesting since we'd left Greece. I didn't say anything about it, but I knew my own demons. When we got off of the plane, a pearl white Maybach with the fishbowl roof was waiting for us, and I ushered her to the back passenger side door. Once I went around and climbed in beside her, I gave the driver the address that we were headed to, and then I shot Jayson a text so that he would know the next move. It took us forty-five minutes to arrive at our destination, but we didn't immediately get out and go in. The closer that we'd gotten to the location, the more nervous she'd gotten, so I wanted to give her a few minutes to get her emotions under control.

"Kwan, you don't have to come in. I can..."

"We've already had this discussion, so let's not waste anymore breath on it," I said, taking her hand in my own.

The smile that she gave me was breathtaking.

"You're making me fall in love with you, you slick muthafucka."

"I'm just returning the favor since I've been putty in your hands from our first run in at the jewelry shop in L.A.," I replied truthfully.

The sound of a powerful engine pulling up fast behind us forced us both to look out the back window, but I had a feeling that I knew who was behind us.

"Is that…"

"No questions, just come on," I said, taking her hand and leading her out of the car.

"What's up, bruh?" Jayson asked, walking toward us.

"Nothing much. It's just time to meet the in laws," I replied.

"Uncle Kenny won't like this," Tink said, standing beside Jayson.

"He may not like it, but he'll definitely understand," I said, holding my hand out.

Jayson slipped me my Sig Sauer 9mm pistol, and I smoothly tucked it in to the back of my shorts. Kyndra looked at me, but not a word of protest left her mouth.

"Let's get this over with," she said.

14

KYNDRA

My heart had been beating wildly in my chest the whole time that we'd been walking up the stairs, but now that I knew that my father was just around the corner, it felt like my heart was stopping. My feet felt like they were cemented into the hardwood of the hallway floor until Kwan squeezed my hand reassuringly. When I looked to my left, he was right there, giving me that lazy smile that melted me like hot butter every single time. I didn't know anybody who could give me confidence in this moment besides my husband, and I was grateful to have him by my side. I gave his hand a squeeze back, took a deep breath, and willed my feet to move again.

"Hey, Daddy," I said, coming around the corner into the downstairs living room.

I'd expected to see my father sitting right where he was, in his favorite chair by the fireplace with a sniffer of brandy in his hand, but I hadn't expected him to have company. I watched as his eyes quickly shifted from me to my entourage and back to me with a new disapproving light enhanced in his pupils by the fireplace's glow.

"Since when do you bring outsiders into a business meeting, Kyndra?" he asked.

"I'd hardly call your son-in-law and his brother outsiders, Uncle Kenny, and you did instruct her to bring him to meet you sooner than later," Tink said.

My father's eyes shifted again, but this time when they landed on Kwan, they lingered long enough for recognition to shine bright and clear. After that happened, I saw something in my father that I'd never witnessed in all my years of living. I saw him become uneasy.

"Daddy, I think you already know my husband, Jakwan."

"Good to see you again, Big Hands," Kwan said.

"H-how-where did you two meet?" he asked, clearly flustered.

"We met in Los Angeles," I replied.

I didn't know why that statement made him smirk, but I caught the expression on his face before he had a chance to conceal it.

"Los Angeles, huh? Well, I'm sure that will make an interesting conversation for another day, but right now, you can excuse Jakwan and his brother so that we can get down to business," he said.

I opened my mouth to speak, but before I could, Kwan had let my hand go and took a step forward.

"I know that you know better than to try and dismiss a real nigga. I'm gonna forgive that disrespect one time off the strength of my wife, but I need you to remember that you knew me before she did."

I didn't know exactly what Kwan's words meant, but I immediately saw the same look of unease creep over my father's features, and something told me that he knew the Kwan that I'd been introduced to when he'd shown me three dead bodies.

"There was no disrespect intended, Kwan, but this is supposed to be a business meeting," he replied evenly.

"Understood, and Kyndra is my business, which means I qualify to be in this room," Kwan stated calmly.

I could feel the temperature rising, and I knew that it had everything to do with my father not being used to being challenged in any way. He was an old school gangster through and through, but he was also the generation that had ushered in Kwan's generation of shooters. That meant that he understood the consequences of disrespect, and I knew that now was my time to step in. I took hold of Kwan's hand and pulled him until he was facing me.

"Just chill on the couch and this shouldn't take long. My dad's not gonna do anything too crazy with company present. You and Jayson just post up," I whispered, staring up into his brown eyes.

I could see the flames of madness burning bright within his iris, but they weren't beyond his control. Not yet.

I had a feeling in the pit of my stomach of what would happen if those flames burned any brighter, and I didn't want that.

"Trust me, bae," I said, giving him a quick peck on the lips and stepping around him.

When I moved, so did Tink, and we didn't stop until we were standing beside my father and his associate.

"What's up, Dad?"

"What's up is that Mr. Wheaton and I would like to know what the hell went wrong and where the cargo is."

"Who are you, Mr. Wheaton?" I asked, trying to understand why this particular white man was entitled to the answers my father was seeking.

"I'm a silent partner of sorts, Ms. Fulher."

"Who he is ain't important because you should already know that he wouldn't be here if he wasn't supposed to be here. Don't get cute," my dad replied, giving me a pointed look that I knew had everything to do with Jayson and Kwan.

I ignored the shot taken and kept the conversation where it needed to be.

"The job went fine except for the fact that the cargo was very different from what was listed on the manifest," I said.

My father's eyes shifted to the couch where I knew Jayson and Kwan were sitting and then back to me. Something told me that for reasons not being made clear to me right now, my father wanted Kwan and his brother as far in the dark as possible.

"We're aware of what the manifest says and what was actually inside the truck. What we don't know is where everything is," Mr. Wheaton stated, sounding more than a little impatient.

"Why weren't we told what to expect?" Tink asked.

"Because you work for me on a need-to-know basis," my dad replied curtly.

"You taught me better than that," I stated coldly.

"Listen, whatever petty squabble you have with dear old dad can wait until later because all that matters right now is the cargo. So, where is it?" Mr. Wheaton asked.

"Watch your tone," Kwan said from across the room.

"Mind your business," my dad said immediately.

The instant shift of the temperature in the room was as obvious as the nose on my face, and I felt Kwan's movement behind me without having to turn around to see it. I felt his hand on my shoulder, and I thought that he was offering me some needed comfort and balance until I saw that his gun was out and up in his right hand.

"Kwan, wait..."

I never got to finish my sentence before the pistol barked, and the bullet hit Mr. Wheaton right in the center of his pale, white forehead. Out of my peripheral, I saw Tink jump in surprise, but my father was smart enough not to move a muscle other than the ones attached to his eyeballs.

"Do you know what you've done?" my dad growled through clenched teeth.

"Of course I do. I'm the one who pulled the trigger," Kwan replied nonchalantly, still not lowering the gun.

"No, dumb nigga, you just killed a Fed," my dad replied, looking at Kwan with a mixture of hatred and contempt.

"Anybody can get it, Big Hands. And I do mean *anybody*," Kwan replied calmly.

They had a staring contest for a few moments before my father conceded defeat, and his withering look was turned on me.

"I hope that you know what the fuck you're doing

because you've just chosen a side other than this family. Get the fuck out of my house and you've got twenty-four hours to turn over my property," he said with so much disgust in his voice.

The shock that I felt left me unable to respond for a second, but that was all the time Kwan needed to turn the gun on my father and level it at his face.

"Don't," I said, putting my hand on Kwan's arm and pushing it down.

I could feel the resistance coursing through his body just by touching him, and I wasn't so sure that my father didn't deserve a bullet, but as his daughter, I couldn't condone it. Not today anyway. Without a word, I took Kwan by the hand and led him back outside to the car.

"Give me the gun," I demanded, holding my hand out.

The questions that suddenly flooded his eyes were evident, but he didn't say a word. He just turned over the pistol to me.

"Tink, get rid of this, and you two need to meet us at the airport," I said, wiping Kwan's prints from the gun with my shirt and passing it off.

"I got you, cuz," Tink replied without hesitation.

"Get in the car, Kwan," I instructed, doing the exact same thing.

Once we were seated side by side, I gave the driver instructions to take us back to the airport.

"I don't run from no nigga, sweetheart, not even your pops," Kwan said.

"You're not running from my father or anyone else. I just need to get to what it is that my dad actually wants."

"So you can give it to him?" Kwan asked.

"Fuck no. We'll just consider it my severance package, but I wanna move it before he realizes where it actually is. Can we still use the plane?" I asked, hopeful.

"Of course."

He pulled out his phone and started making arrangements immediately, which gave me a few minutes to contemplate what my next move would be. A part of me had always known that I'd have to tell Kwan my secrets one day, but I hadn't imagined or anticipated that he would get caught up in my shit before I could fully explain. Now it seemed like more than an explanation was due. I reached over and pushed the button that sent the partition up to separate us from the driver, and then I turned in my seat to face him.

"We need to talk," I said, feeling queasy in my stomach.

He didn't say anything, but he turned to demonstrate that I had his undivided attention.

"You've dealt with my father, so you know that his business isn't always on the up and up."

"I'm aware. And from the tone of that conversation that took place back there, I think that it's a safe assumption that you were involved in something less than legal," he said, nodding understandingly.

"Yeah, I was. We were supposed to hit three tractor trailers coming out of Mexico traveling up the West Coast, and they were supposed to be full of fentanyl."

The fact that he laughed at the information that I'd just divulged caught me completely by surprise and had me looking at him like he was losing his mind.

"So, wait, are you telling me that you actually pulled

off robbing the cartel convoy?" he asked, looking at me somewhat skeptically.

"You say that like it's impossible to believe or like the cartel can't get touched."

"Oh, no, I'm aware that anyone can get touched, sweetheart. I also know that it takes a certain type of individual to reach and touch an animal that dangerous, which means that I've severely underestimated you," he replied, smiling at me with a strange sense of pride.

"Well, let me finish before you give me my flowers because there's more to the story. Only one of the trucks was full of fentanyl. The other two had gold and platinum bars in them."

This part of my revelation caused the smile to fall completely off of his face, and a look of concern that was so sincere replaced it. My heart was instantly beating harder.

"Gold and platinum bars? You're sure about that?" he asked softly.

"Yeah, I'm sure, Kwan. I was there. I saw the shit with my own eyes. Why?" I asked, getting an increasingly bad feeling.

"A while ago, I'd heard a rumor about a new method that the cartel had for washing their money and that they were getting help from the U.S. government. I never got the full story, and something like that ain't what you ask about if you don't got shit to do with it. What you just describes sounds about right though."

"Which would also explain why a Fed was sitting in my father's living room," I said, doing the math now.

"I'd bet that he wasn't just any Fed. He had to have ties

to the treasury department because you're talking about a lot of money in gold and platinum."

"Okay, but what I don't understand is why any government official would be involved with the cartel," I said.

"Because this country is built off of blood money, exploitation, and the art of criminal enterprise. Not to mention, the insatiable greed of the U.S. government. Paper money doesn't appreciate in value in the U.S. like it does in foreign countries because we're the one printing the money. Just like precious metals and jewels don't mean as much in third world countries because they're the ones in the mines full of the shit. So, in this case, an even swap ain't no swindle, which means the convoy that you jacked was more than likely repayment of money already funneled to the cartel," he explained.

"But bae, everybody knows that cartels use their money and resources to continue fighting the narco wars against their government and to pay for more corruption."

"You say that like the U.S. ain't known for funding wars or sticking their nose in business that don't got shit to do with them," he replied with a straight face.

His point made me feel extremely naïve about the world I'd been living and operating in, but it also made me understand the magnitude of what me and my crew had done.

"How much of this do you think my dad knows?" I asked.

The look that he gave me was a sympathetic one, but it didn't hide the truth that I really didn't wanna face about my own father's willingness to put his only daughter in harm's way for the money. No matter how much money we stood to make.

"I'm sorry, sweetheart."

Kwan took my hand and just being here with him made me feel better than if I'd been facing this shit on my own. I knew that I didn't have all of the answers right now, if for no other reason than for the fact that I didn't have all the pieces to the puzzle. I knew that I was married to a strong, capable man who I'd obviously underestimated too, and I was grateful beyond words for that.

"What do you think that I need to do next?" I asked.

He gave the question some thought for several moments, and it was fascinating for me to see how this part of his brain worked.

"Well, me shooting dude obviously didn't make the situation any better, but I'm not especially worried about that part right now. The best move right now is to hide what you jacked and then fall off the face of the earth. Is it hidden in a safe enough spot?"

"I don't know. I mean, right now, all three trucks that I used to switch and carry the loads are parked in Montana on private property. I'd like to move them just in case my father found out somehow, but I don't even have drivers right now. I had to shoot the last ones because I couldn't trust them not to double cross me for that type of come up," I confessed.

"Okay, we'll get you some drivers to move it, and I want you to take it to the airport for transport because the safest place is somewhere we own that lacks extradition."

I smiled immediately because I knew just where he was talking about. I listened as he called Jayson and instructed him to have two people named Blaze and Fabian get to Montana to help, and then we'd all meet up in Greece.

"Where are you going?" I asked as soon as he hung up the phone.

"I gotta make a quick run to D.C., but trust me, I'll be multitasking the whole time. We need all of the facts in order to properly assess the threat."

15

KWAN

Washington, D.C.

"Took your ass long enough to get here," she said, sounding both weak and tired.

"I figured that you'd be tired of hospital food, so I had to stop and get your favorite," I replied, holding up the Styrofoam tray in my hand for her to see.

"If that's chicken and mumbo sauce then I might not have a choice except to forgive you."

"Heavy on the mumbo sauce," I said, crossing the room and sitting the food on the tray table in front of her.

From her semi seated position, she popped open the lid on the tray and inhaled deeply with her eyes closed, giving the impression that she was communing with God in thanks. When she opened her eyes, I thought that she was gonna get right to the business of fucking the chicken up, but instead, she closed the tray and just laid back.

"You mean to tell me that you're not hungry?" I asked, pulling up a chair beside her bed and sitting down.

"Honestly, I haven't really had much of an appetite or been able to sleep."

Instead of offering her any type of hollow platitude, I just took her hand in mine and kissed the back of it gently.

"I'm glad that you survived," I said genuinely.

When she looked at me, her eyes instantly filled with tears that ran over onto her cheeks and down her beautiful face, creating a mask of anguish.

"Part of me wishes that I hadn't survived... But I understand that this was my instant karma, and there's no escaping that," she said sadly.

"No, this ain't your karma, sweetheart. I refuse to believe that you of all people has done anything in this life that would earn you three bullets."

"That's because you don't understand the whole story," she replied.

The look of guilt that suddenly contorted her features was thoroughly confusing, but I was content to let her talk through whatever she was feeling.

"What don't I understand, Rashawna? We don't know that those three shots were even meant for you."

"Well, given the fact that you ain't got so much as a scratch on you and the gun barrel never moved off of me, I'd say that we have enough conclusive evidence to say those shots were meant for me," she replied dryly.

"Okay, well, being a federal judge comes with risk. That still don't make this shit karma though."

"You're right, Kwan... but losing the baby like that,

with you right there, that's how I know that it was my instant karma."

"I don't understand," I replied, giving her a confused look.

For a moment, she looked away and tried to pull her hand away from mine, but I tightened my grip. I'd been afraid to ask if she knew about the baby, but realistically, I knew that she understood that her taking two bullets to the chest and one to the stomach made her own survival miraculous. Her child surviving, that would've been some amazing work by God, and I somehow needed to convince her that this wasn't God's punishment simply because she didn't understand its purpose right now.

"Kwan, I lied to you."

"About what and when?" I asked, still confused but intrigued.

"I lied to you when I said that the baby wasn't yours. It wasn't that I was trying to keep your child from you or anything. I just wanted you and your wife to have a fresh start without the stereotypical baby mama shit," she explained, looking at me with eyes full of an immeasurable pain and regret as her tears continued to fall.

My words got stuck in my throat, making it an effort to swallow the massive truth that she'd just dropped on me. My emotions were spinning fast enough to make me feel like the room was in motion too, and for a split second, I thought that I was gonna pass out from sensory overload. What she'd said made sense, but I still had the desire to question her right to make that type of decision about a child that was both of ours. The real nigga in me knew that I'd only be causing more harm and guilt, and I had too much love for her to add to her grief in that way. So, instead, I squeezed her hand tighter to offer more comfort and support.

"I understand you wanting to give me a fresh start, but I need you to always remember that no relationship can erase everything that we've meant to each other for all of these years. I wouldn't want that, nor would I allow that to happen, because you're a part of my soul tribe. Never forget that," I said, meaning every word.

"You're not mad at me?"

"There's no room for anger, sweetheart, because we're both grieving this loss and lashing out at each other only dishonors our child's memory," I replied.

"Thank you for that... But Kwan, I know you, so I know the rage that you'll eventually let yourself feel will be directed somewhere, at someone. Please don't do anything because I can't lose you now."

I wanted to promise her that this fear she was expressing wouldn't manifest, but my mind flashed with images of Mr. Wheaton's life ending by my hand. Not to mention that whoever was responsible for my child now being with the angels had a debt to be settled too.

"You're not gonna lose me...but I'm gonna have to disappear for a while," I said.

"Why?" she asked, wiping the tears from her face and sitting up a little more in the bed.

"How much do you really wanna know?"

"That question alone tells me that I need to know everything, so spit it out before I get mad," she replied.

"Do you know a Fed by the last name of Wheaton?" I asked, watching her expression closely.

"I don't know him personally, but if we're talking about the same guy then he works on the administrative team at the federal reserve."

I took a moment to digest this information, not that it surprised me at all.

"Okay, so long story short, I had to kill him earlier today, but it's because he definitely had dirt under his fingernails," I replied.

"Were there any witnesses?"

"None that will tell, but the reason that I killed him is why I gotta lay low for a while. Unbeknownst to me, he was part of an elaborate robbery, and what was taken is gonna bring out some head hunters," I explained.

It was her turn to just stare at me for a moment and process what I was saying, and I could see the wheels of suspicion turning behind her bright eyes.

"I get a feeling that this ain't about the same robbery that we discussed the last time that I saw you, and if Wheaton was involved, then you're talking about possible high level government corruption. So, it would seem that your enemies are getting more formidable, and that's making me question whether or not you have a death wish."

"Absolutely not. I promise you that I didn't know this Wheaton guy before today, and I instinctively knew that he couldn't be trusted," I replied.

"Kwan, with the type of enemies that you're making, I don't think that you can trust anybody. I mean, think about it. It takes a special type of muthafucka to be able to withstand serious pressure, and what you're talking about is beyond serious. Trust is a luxury that you can no longer afford."

The truth in her words imbedded itself in my brain like sage wisdom delivered by a veteran at this street shit. Rashawna wasn't in the streets, but her advantage was in having to navigate the political cesspool in D.C. every single day.

"Listen, I can handle this situation, but I'm more worried about you. I've played back the shooting more times than I can count, and more and more, you look like the intended target. I need to know who would want to kill you because this wasn't instant karma," I said seriously.

"I'm a judge, so I'm sure that a lot of muthafuckas want me dead."

The answer that she gave was one that I could accept because it was logical, and I'd thought along the same lines. But in this moment, the conversation that I'd had with Jayson, Fabian, and Blaze was playing in the background to my thoughts like annoying elevator music. I thought I was content to let it go, but I knew that after everything I'd learned about Kyndra and her father, I had to have this conversation with Rashawna.

"I need to ask you something. How well did you know Michael Newcome?" I asked.

"The NFL quarterback that was murdered by his wife? I knew him well enough, I guess. We met in college and kept in touch afterwards. I've been to dinner and different functions with him and his wife since he started playing for the Washington Commanders. Why are you asking me about him?"

"Because I need to know if he came to you and asked

you for help due to him being extorted after he was robbed," I replied.

"Please don't tell me that you had anything to do with that, Kwan, because he was my friend, and that shit ultimately led to his death," she said, looking at me with even more pain in her eyes.

"No, I wasn't involved in that at all, but it's possible that the reason you got shot had to do with you helping him. So, were you looking into the situation?"

"I mean, yeah, but I'd only put out a few feelers on how to annul the sale of his real estate holding company. That was all that he really cared about, and I understood given the portfolio he'd already put together. He had a house in New York, two in Malibu, along with a one hundred thirty acre ranch in Montana that he'd built a mansion on. Whoever forced him to sign those papers made a serious come up," she replied.

As she was explaining herself, there was a part of me that remained skeptical, but that vanished the moment she mentioned the property in Montana. Coincidence was something that real street niggas didn't believe in, so the fact that Kyndra owned property there was all the confirmation that I needed. Now, the question was what would I do with this information because it literally changed everything. It was highly probable that my new wife had directly — or indirectly — caused the death of my first child.

"Kwan, are you okay?"

Before I could answer, I heard my phone ring, and I used the distraction of answering it to gather my thoughts somewhat.

"Hello?"

"It's Fabian, and we have a problem."

"What's the problem?" I asked.

"There's no way that we can get everything in those trucks onto the plane, so I hope you've got a backup plan," he replied.

For a moment, I didn't because I'd already anticipated things moving according to the first plan. Life was all about the ability to adjust though.

"Get the trucks to the nearest airport and arrange for transport that way. If you have to buy an international cargo ship then do that but do whatever it takes to move everything."

"Okay, I got it," he replied.

"One more thing though. I want you to check sales records for Michael Newcome's real estate company. A transaction like that requires a paper trail and a notary, so I need a name," I said, looking at Rashawna.

"That shouldn't be too hard to find. I'll text you the info when I have it."

I disconnected the call, but my gaze never wavered from hers, and I could feel her thinking as she tried to put the pieces of this particular puzzle together.

"What aren't you telling me?" she asked.

"That's a broad question, so maybe you could narrow it down just a little."

"I get the strange feeling that you have a working idea of who was behind the robbery and extortion, which means that you think you know who shot me. Am I wrong?" she asked, giving me a look that dared me to lie to her.

"You're not wrong, but I can't give you any details because I'm gonna handle this my way."

"Kwan, your way means that somebody dies."

"It won't be anyone that doesn't deserve it," I stated coldly.

"I know that you're hurting, because I'm hurting too, but you can't kill in our child's name."

"I think you mean that I *shouldn't* kill in our child's name because we both know that I can and will do anything I want," I stated.

"Kwan, please. If something happens to you..."

"Nothing is gonna happen to me. I promise," I said, taking her hand in mine.

The worry in her eyes made them shine brighter than ever, but I also saw the trust that she had in me and my word. I didn't truly know how I was gonna play this situation because it gave a whole new meaning to the word delicate. Handling it with care was a necessity.

"Are you gonna tell me who it is that did this?" she asked.

"No, because I want you to always be able to maintain plausible deniability and your integrity as an officer of the court."

She nodded in understanding and resignation, but part of me felt guilt for not speaking the truth about my unwillingness to disclose my wife's probable involvement. I just didn't see what good would be done by telling Rashawna about the unintentional collision between our past and my present because it wasn't something that would promote closure. It would only breed the insatiable hunger for revenge. When my phone vibrated in my hand, I looked at the screen and read the text message from Fabian. After a moment of thought, I typed one word with a question mark, and then I waited. A few seconds later, the requested information popped up along with a picture of the woman I would be looking for. Her vague familiarity fed my anger. I committed both to memory, and then I slid my phone back into my pocket.

"I gotta go," I said, standing up and placing a kiss on her forehead.

"Please be careful, Kwan. Risking your life or having your life taken isn't gonna bring our baby back."

"I know. All that I can do now is restore the balance in the universe," I replied, letting her hand go as I turned to leave the room.

I could feel her reluctance to let me leave, but she didn't call me back. By the time that I made it downstairs to my black BMW 900i, my mind was made up about how I would handle the next part of this mission. I made a couple phone calls to set things in motion, and then I headed across the bridge into Virginia to the address that I'd been given. It was about forty-five minutes later when my car crept to a stop on a sleepy tree lined street of a suburban neighborhood in West Springfield, Virginia. It wasn't too late at night, but it was obvious that there wasn't a lot of action to be had in these parts. I was sitting in my car, trying to strategize how best to get Skylar Collins to come outside of her plush townhouse, when her front door opened ten yards away from me. She exited carrying a duffle bag over her shoulder, and she seemed to be preoccupied with thoughts. It was clear to see that her intentions were to slide behind the wheel of her new Mercedes E class SUV sitting in front of her house, and that was what made me hop out of my car quick.

"Ms. Collins?" I called, walking toward her nonchalantly.

The curious look that she gave me never made it to full blown suspicion before my gun was out and pointed at her.

"Wh-what do you want?" she asked shakily.

"Something that you can't give. So, I guess that your life will have to suffice."

16

KYNDRA

Santorini
One Day Later

I couldn't explain the restlessness that was robbing me of my sleep, but when I looked at the clock for what felt like the hundredth time, only to see that it was 4 am, I gave up. I got out of bed and decided to take a blistering hot shower to hopefully decompress and release the built up tension in my body. It wasn't until I stepped from beneath the water's spray thirty minutes later that I fully realized that my restlessness was due to my extreme mental fatigue and not anything to do with my body. Going from New York to Montana to Greece would've worn anybody out physically, but so far, I'd been awake for more than twenty-four hours.

As I was drying off and putting on a pair of panties to match one of Kwan's t-shirts that I loved sleeping in, my subconscious spoke up and told me the real truth about the source of my restlessness. It was my husband. One would think that the precious cargo that we had on the high seas headed in this direction would cause severe anxiety because it was out of sight and out of my control. The reality was that I hadn't given the cargo a second thought. The fact that I hadn't heard from Kwan since we'd split up in New York was what had me worried and sick to my stomach. I'd called him repeatedly but got no answer, and my text messages were left on read. When I questioned Jayson, he just kept assuring me that Kwan was fine, just handling sensitive business that required his full attention. Part of me completely understood that, but it was my instincts and not my business savvy mind screaming at me that something was wrong. Really wrong. By the time we'd actually touched down in Santorini, I'd been calling Skylar with the intent of having her track Kwan's movements, but she hadn't answered. I wasn't that worried about her though because I knew that she would've dumped her phone like Tink and I had, so her silence was more than likely due to her not having a new one yet. All of that added up to me having to be patient, which wasn't anywhere near being one of my strong suits. When I came back into the bedroom from out of the master bathroom, it took every ounce of my remaining willpower not to pick up my phone and check it or call Kwan again. As badly as I simply wanted to hear his voice, I knew the risks that I posed to his safety if I became the thing that distracted him at an inopportune time. So instead of going for my phone, I grabbed a pre-rolled blunt from the nightstand and took it outside on the balcony to smoke.

"You can't sleep either, huh?" Tink asked.

I jumped at the sound of her voice and squinted in the direction that it had come from. After a few moments, her silhouette came into focus.

"Bitch, why are you sitting out here in the dark?" I asked in a fierce whisper.

"Obviously because I can't sleep either, bitch."

"Where's Jayson?" I asked, looking down the long, wraparound, top tier balcony in the direction of the room they shared.

"He's sleep... or at least pretending to be sleep."

That statement made me sit down next to her and light the blunt.

"Why would he ever pretend to be asleep?" I asked, blowing out a stream of smoke.

"I don't know. He's just been acting weird ever since we got here. I keep asking him what's going on, but he's saying that it's nothing. It don't feel like nothing."

The worry that I heard in her voice matched my own feelings but for different reasons. I passed her the blunt and let her fill her lungs before I spoke again.

"Give me an example of some weird shit that's happened," I said.

"Okay, like the sex. I ain't even gon hold you, cuz. That nigga know how to tear my muthafuckin framework apart and have me gagging for it. Like I don't get *enough*. Normally, he's down for the pound whatever, whenever, but lately, I can't get shit except for a quickie," she replied, shaking her head in obvious disappointment.

"Okay, have you two been arguing or fighting about anything?"

"That's the thing. I *don't* argue with this man! I be on some 'yes, Daddy' shit for real," she said, getting animated.

I gave her the hand signal for her to quiet the fuck down and give me my blunt back because it was obvious that she was already turnt. When I put the blunt back to my lips, I tasted the Hennessey that had obviously been transferred by her, and that alone told me just how serious this issue was between her and Jayson.

"When did he first start acting weird?" I asked.

"Remember when I told you that he was asking me shit about the NFL quarterback? Well, shit ain't really been the same since then, but it's not so blatant that I would say that he ain't fucking wit me."

"So, then what would you say it's like?" I asked.

She got quiet for a moment, and even in the dark, she was thinking about how to describe it to me.

"I guess I just feel like he's looking at me with the side eye. Almost like he knows more about me than he's saying."

As I hit the blunt again, I had a sudden illuminating thought that could either be blamed on the weed or me just finally seeing the nose on my face.

"I'd say that it's a safe bet that he knows more than he's saying, especially after the shit show at my dad's spot. Kwan and I had a deep conversation about my dad prior to the meeting, and I know the pieces came together for him about our double life that night. Did you and Jayson talk about it?"

"Nah, not for real. We just got straight to the business of trying to secure everything before your dad found out where we were hiding the shit. Now that you mention it though, we learned some shit about Kwan and Jayson too," she pointed out.

"What do you mean?"

"For starters, I ain't never seen nobody bring out the ho in Uncle Kenny, but it was obvious that he didn't really want no parts of Kwan. They were more than a little familiar with each other, which means that they've done dirt together, and you already know that Jayson is Kwan's righthand. So then, they're obviously in the street more than either of us realized, " she concluded.

"Okay, I'm following you, but how's that any different from us?" I asked, playing the devil's advocate.

"That's exactly what I'm saying to you. So now, think about everything that we know and have learned and tell me that you don't look at that night at the gallery in L.A. differently."

"Oh, my God!... bitchhhh," I whispered, feeling like the smartest dumb bitch alive.

It was like someone had turned on the world's brightest light, and now I could see everywhere that had been dark before. Surprisingly, I wasn't mad though because the criminal mastermind in me respected the hustle and genius it had taken to pull that move off and vanish like ghosts.

"Them niggas are good," I said, chuckling.

"Right! I'm over here imagining what type of unstop-pable force we could all be together. We'd be more powerful than the old mafia niggas in New York back in the day."

"You're right. We could be... but I don't know because, honestly, I've been thinking about settling down, maybe giving my nigga a few kids," I said, finishing the blunt and tossing the roach.

I expected her to have some wild outburst about what I'd just dropped on her, but she was uncharacteristically quiet.

"Tink, you good?"

"Huh? Oh, yeah, I was thinking about what you said, and it made me wonder what type of mother I'mma be," she replied.

"Gonna be? Bitch, are you trying to tell me something?"

"Ain't nothing to tell as of right now. I mean, Jayson and I ain't never used a condom, and I been stopped taking my birth control because I wasn't scared to have a baby with him. I know that sounds crazy as fuck," she said, chuckling softly.

"Actually, it don't sound crazy at all."

While we'd been sitting around, kicking the shit, the sky had lightened up in preparation of the rising sun, so we could see each other's facial expression a little clearer now. When she saw mine, she burst out laughing.

"You muthafuckin slut puppy you! Do you got something that you wanna tell me?" she asked.

"The only thing that I got to tell you is that a bitch got the munchies, and we need to go raid the kitchen right the fuck now," I replied, standing up and pulling her to her feet.

"I'm wit you, cuz."

I led the way in from the balcony through my room and downstairs to the kitchen. When I hit the switch to turn on the lights, I immediately jumped backwards, screaming, almost knocking Tink over.

"K-Kwan, is that you? When did you get home?" I asked, trying to calm my racing heart.

"About an hour ago," he replied calmly.

His voice sounded normal, but the look in his eyes was somehow... off. Along with this revelation was when I noticed that Jayson was sitting at the kitchen table with Kwan, and both of them had guns laid out in front of them.

"What's going on?" I asked, stepping to the side a little so that Tink could see what I saw.

"Both of you come take a seat because we need to talk about some things," Jayson said.

My entire body was screaming at me not to move, but logically, I knew that neither one of us had anything to fear from these men. I found my hand back inside of Tink's, and then we proceeded to move forward to the kitchen table. It wasn't until I sat down and got a good look at Kwan that I saw the blood covering his shirt, face, and neck.

"Baby, what happened?" I asked calmly, fighting against the hysteria that wanted to rip through my throat.

"We'll get to that, but there's a more pressing conversation that we need to have," Kwan replied.

"Nothing is more pressing than getting you help if you're hurt, bae, so please…"

"The blood ain't his," Jayson said, interrupting me.

"Whose is it?" Tink asked.

"Patience, Tink, patience," Jayson replied, smiling.

"Kwan, what the fuck is going on?" I asked, making the swift transition from concerned to angry.

"That's what I've been trying to figure out, sweetheart. After I left you and went back to check on my friend in D.C., I kinda stumbled upon some info that my crew had pitched to me as a 'hypothetical' before I brought you to Greece the first time. We'd been trying to figure out who'd taken a shot at me... and hit Rashawna by mistake."

As soon as my brain had registered the name that had just leapt off of his tongue, I felt my mouth fall open, and I knew my expression was a dead giveaway. My brain was searching for words, but nothing coherent was sliding into place to help a bitch out right about now.

"I can tell that you're familiar with the name, but you're obviously trying to process how I came to know this particular female. Allow me to fill in some gaps. When you insisted that I clean house and put women on notice that I was officially off the market, there was only one woman to notify. I've known Rashawna for almost a decade, and we'd been fucking around that long, so I felt like she deserved a face-to-face breakup. We ended up going to lunch... And you know the rest. What you couldn't possibly know was that she was pregnant, and she'd actually told me that right after I'd told her that I was married. She told me that the baby wasn't mine, and I believed her, but after she was shot, she told me the truth... And we tried to grieve our baby that would never be born."

"Oh, shit," Tink said, putting her hands up to her face.

My thoughts went from shock to devastation before they finally turned fearful because the reality of what he was saying hit home like a hollow point. We'd killed his baby.

"Kwan-Kwan, I'm so sorry, baby. I swear to you that I didn't know, and I'm so sorry," I said, swiping at the tears cascading down my face.

"You didn't know what?" Jayson asked.

"We didn't know that Rashawna Goode had any type of ties to you," Tink replied.

"Who pulled the trigger?" Kwan asked.

"I didn't," I replied quickly.

"Neither did I," Tink said.

"That wasn't the question that was asked. The question was who pulled the trigger?" Kwan asked, speaking in a slow, forceful tone that signaled the onset of homicidal madness.

I didn't know what the truth would cost me and Tink right now, but I was pretty damn certain of the price of a lie. The fact that Skylar wasn't here yet made the decision for me.

"I-I don't know who pulled the trigger. That part was arranged by my other business associate," I replied.

"Oh, you mean Skylar?" Kwan asked.

"How did you know that?" Tink asked.

"Because we're good at what we do," Jayson replied, sneering at her like he wanted to spit in her face.

When my eyes moved back to Kwan, I couldn't get a read on what he was thinking or feeling, and that only made me more fearful.

"Baby, nothing can excuse what happened, and I promise you that if I'd had known that Rashawna was at all connected to you, I would've come to you and asked for your help. You know how my father is, and when he says that a situation has to be dealt with, it's nonnegotiable."

"Oh, so it was your father's decision?" Kwan asked.

"Yeah. He found out that Michael Newcome had gone to the judge for help to undo what we'd done, and he gave me instructions to clean up the mess," I admitted.

Kwan and Jayson exchanged a look before Jayson picked up his pistol off of the table, stood up, and left the room without a word.

"I want you to know that I believe you, Kyndra. I believe that your dad gave the order that you couldn't refuse, and I believe that Skylar made sure that the job was complete. In fact, she drove the car during the drive-by, and I know that firsthand. None of that changes the fact that someone I care about was shot and left for dead, nor the fact that my first conceived child perished as a senseless casualty. So, how do we fix that, sweetheart? How can I be made whole again?" he asked patiently.

"I-I don't know that you can be made whole," I replied honestly.

"No... I guess you're right."

Before I could offer any type of plea or more apologies, Jayson reentered the room, escorting a badly beaten man who resembled my father.

"Oh, God. Daddy," I moaned, putting my hand to my mouth.

"I'm-I'm okay, Kyndra," he mumbled through a clearly broken jaw.

Jayson roughly shoved him down into a chair beside Tink, across from Kwan, and then he went to the refrigerator.

"Oh, my God!" Tink screamed.

When I looked over at Jayson, he was carrying a severed head that he placed in the middle of the kitchen table like it was a frosted beer mug. The look of permanent anguish on Skylar's face forced the vomit up past my windpipe, causing me to turn my head and become violently ill all over the floor.

"That's not very ladylike," Kwan said, chuckling humorlessly.

When I was finally able to look back up at him, his hand was resting on the pistol in front of him.

"Kwan, please," I begged.

"Please what? Please don't kill you? Sweetheart, what type of husband do you think I am?" he asked, sounding genuinely wounded.

"Then wh-what are you gonna do?" I asked.

"I'm not gonna do anything. You are," he replied, pushing the gun across the table to me.

"Huh?" I asked, confused.

"Everybody who played a part has to pay a price. So, you have to choose, right here, right now, to either kill your father or your cousin. If you don't choose, and execute, one of them, then Jayson will be forced to choose for you. I have a feeling that he's gonna choose to kill both of them though."

"Kwan, wait..."

"There's one bullet in the chamber, sweetheart, so who's it gonna be?" Kwan asked.

"Wait, Kwan, please!" I cried.

"Sixty seconds," Kwan said, looking at his watch.

I wanted so bad for him to be joking, but my dead friend's severed head told me just how serious he was. There was no mercy in his eyes, and that meant that there was no easy way out of this.

"Thirty seconds," Kwan stated.

It felt like I couldn't breathe, and my heart hurt so bad... but I knew what I had to do. So, I picked up the gun... and I chose.

To be continued...

.

Assisted Publishing Packages

BASIC PACKAGE

$699

Editing

Cover Design

Formatting

UPGRADED PACKAGE

$1,000

Typing

Editing

Cover Design

Formatting

ADVANCE PACKAGE

$1,400

Typing

Editing

Cover Design

Formatting

Copyright registration

Proofreading

Upload book to Amazon

LDP SUPREME PACKAGE

$1,700

Typing

Editing

Cover Design

Formatting

Copyright registration

Proofreading

Set up Amazon account

Upload book to Amazon

Advertise on LDP, Amazon and Facebook Page

Submission Guidelines

Submit the first three chapters of your completed manuscript to ldpsubmissions@gmail.com. In the subject line add Your Book's Title. The manuscript must be in a Word Doc file and sent as an attachment. Document should be in Times New Roman, double spaced, and in size 12 font. Also, provide your synopsis and full contact information. If sending multiple submissions, they must each be in a separate email.

Have a story but no way to send it electronically? You can still submit to LDP/Ca$h Presents. Send in the first three chapters, written or typed, of your completed manuscript to:

LDP: Submissions Dept
P.O. Box 944
Stockbridge, GA 30281-9998

DO NOT send original manuscript. Must be a duplicate.
Provide your synopsis and a cover letter containing your full contact information.

Thanks for considering LDP and Ca$h Presents.

NEW RELEASES

BLOODLINE OF A SAVAGE 1&2
THESE VICIOUS STREETS 1&2
RELENTLESS GOON
RELENTLESS GOON 2
BY PRINCE A. TAUHID

THE BUTTERFLY MAFIA 1-3
BY FUMIYA PAYNE

A THUG'S STREET PRINCESS 1&2
BY MEESHA

CITY OF SMOKE 2
BY MOLOTTI

STEPPERS 1,2&3
THE REAL BADDIES OF CHI-RAQ
BY KING RIO

THE LANE 1&2
BY KEN-KEN SPENCE

THUG OF SPADES 1&2
LOVE IN THE TRENCHES 2
CORNER BOYS
BY COREY ROBINSON

TIL DEATH 3

BY ARYANNA

THE BIRTH OF A GANGSTER 4
BY DELMONT PLAYER

PRODUCT OF THE STREETS 1&2
BY DEMOND "MONEY" ANDERSON

NO TIME FOR ERROR
BY KEESE

MONEY HUNGRY DEMONS
BY TRANAY ADAMS

STANDING ON HER BUSINESS 2
BY DG SANTANA

TENDER
BY KHUFU

HUB CITY MENACE
BY JAQUILLE M. WHITE

COUNTDOWN TO A KILLA
CLOCK'S TICKING
BY LO-LIFE

FO'EVA ROLLIN'
BY ASSA RAYMOND BAKER

THUG OF SPADES 3

BY COREY ROBINSON

THE PLUG'S RUTHLESS DAUGHTER 2
BY TONY DANIELS

DYING FOR LIKES
KILLING AIN'T A GAME
BY ARYANNA

GET IT IN SLUGS
BY B STALL

BLOODY MONEY BAGS
VIOLENT LOVE
BY KINGPEN

KILLA CREW
WHAT'S MINE IS YOURS
BY ARYANNA

Coming Soon from Lock Down Publications/Ca$h Presents

IF YOU CROSS ME ONCE 6
ANGEL V
By Anthony Fields

IMMA DIE BOUT MINE 5
By Aryanna

A THUGS STREET PRINCESS 3
By Meesha

PRODUCT OF THE STREETS 3
By Demond Money Anderson

CORNER BOYS 2
By Corey Robinson

THE MURDER QUEENS 6&7
By Michael Gallon

CITY OF SMOKE 3
By Molotti

CONFESSIONS OF A DOPE BOY
By Nicholas Lock

THA TAKEOVER
By Keith Chandler

BETRAYAL OF A G 2
By Ray Vinci

CRIME BOSS
By Playa Ray

Available Now

RESTRAINING ORDER 1 & 2
By CA$H & Coffee

LOVE KNOWS NO BOUNDARIES 1-3
By Coffee

RAISED AS A GOON I, II, III & IV
BRED BY THE SLUMS I, II, III
BLAST FOR ME I & II
ROTTEN TO THE CORE I II III
A BRONX TALE I, II, III
DUFFLE BAG CARTEL I II III IV V VI
HEARTLESS GOON I II III IV V
A SAVAGE DOPEBOY I II
DRUG LORDS I II III
CUTTHROAT MAFIA I II
KING OF THE TRENCHES
By Ghost

LAY IT DOWN I & II
LAST OF A DYING BREED I II
BLOOD STAINS OF A SHOTTA I & II III
By Jamaica

LOYAL TO THE GAME I II III
LIFE OF SIN I, II III
By TJ & Jelissa

IF LOVING HIM IS WRONG…I & II
LOVE ME EVEN WHEN IT HURTS I II III
By Jelissa

PUSH IT TO THE LIMIT
By Bre' Hayes

BLOODY COMMAS I & II
SKI MASK CARTEL I, II & III
KING OF NEW YORK I II, III IV V
RISE TO POWER I II III
COKE KINGS I II III IV V
BORN HEARTLESS I II III IV
KING OF THE TRAP I II
By T.J. Edwards

WHEN THE STREETS CLAP BACK I & II III
THE HEART OF A SAVAGE I II III IV
MONEY MAFIA I II
LOYAL TO THE SOIL I II III
By Jibril Williams

A DISTINGUISHED THUG STOLE MY HEART I
II & III
LOVE SHOULDN'T HURT I II III IV
RENEGADE BOYS 1-4
PAID IN KARMA 1-3

SAVAGE STORMS 1-3
AN UNFORESEEN LOVE 1-3
BABY, I'M WINTERTIME COLD 1-3
A THUG'S STREET PRINCESS 1&2
By Meesha

A GANGSTER'S CODE 1-3
A GANGSTER'S SYN 1-3
THE SAVAGE LIFE 1-3
CHAINED TO THE STREETS 1-3
BLOOD ON THE MONEY 1-3
A GANGSTA'S PAIN 1-3
BEAUTIFUL LIES AND UGLY TRUTHS
CHURCH IN THESE STREETS
By J-Blunt

CUM FOR ME 1-8
An LDP Erotica Collaboration

BLOOD OF A BOSS 1-5
SHADOWS OF THE GAME
TRAP BASTARD
By Askari

THE STREETS BLEED MURDER 1-3
THE HEART OF A GANGSTA 1-3
By Jerry Jackson

WHEN A GOOD GIRL GOES BAD
By Adrienne

THE COST OF LOYALTY 1-3
By Kweli

BRIDE OF A HUSTLA 1-3
THE FETTI GIRLS 1-3
CORRUPTED BY A GANGSTA 1-4
BLINDED BY HIS LOVE
THE PRICE YOU PAY FOR LOVE 1-3
DOPE GIRL MAGIC 1-3
By Destiny Skai

A KINGPIN'S AMBITION
A KINGPIN'S AMBITION II
I MURDER FOR THE DOUGH
By Ambitious

TRUE SAVAGE 1-7
DOPE BOY MAGIC 1-3
MIDNIGHT CARTEL 1-3
CITY OF KINGZ 1&2
NIGHTMARE ON SILENT AVE
THE PLUG OF LIL MEXICO 1&2
CLASSIC CITY
By Chris Green

A GANGSTER'S REVENGE 1-4
THE BOSS MAN'S DAUGHTERS 1-5
A SAVAGE LOVE 1&2
BAE BELONGS TO ME 1&2
A HUSTLER'S DECEIT 1-3
WHAT BAD BITCHES DO 1-3

SOUL OF A MONSTER 1-3
KILL ZONE
A DOPE BOY'S QUEEN 1-3
TIL DEATH 1-3
IMMA DIE BOUT MINE 1-4
By Aryanna

A DOPEBOY'S PRAYER
By Eddie "Wolf" Lee

THE KING CARTEL 1-3
By Frank Gresham

THESE NIGGAS AIN'T LOYAL 1-3
By Nikki Tee

GANGSTA SHYT 1-3
By CATO

THE ULTIMATE BETRAYAL
By Phoenix

BOSS'N UP 1-3
By Royal Nicole

I LOVE YOU TO DEATH
By Destiny J

I RIDE FOR MY HITTA
I STILL RIDE FOR MY HITTA
By Misty Holt

LOVE & CHASIN' PAPER
By Qay Crockett

TO DIE IN VAIN
SINS OF A HUSTLA
By ASAD

BROOKLYN HUSTLAZ
By Boogsy Morina

BROOKLYN ON LOCK 1 & 2
By Sonovia

GANGSTA CITY
By Teddy Duke

A DRUG KING AND HIS DIAMOND 1-3
A DOPEMAN'S RICHES
HER MAN, MINE'S TOO 1&2
CASH MONEY HO'S
THE WIFEY I USED TO BE 1&2
PRETTY GIRLS DO NASTY THINGS
By Nicole Goosby

LIPSTICK KILLAH 1-3
CRIME OF PASSION 1-3
FRIEND OR FOE 1-3
By Mimi

TRAPHOUSE KING 1-3
KINGPIN KILLAZ 1-3

STREET KINGS 1&2
PAID IN BLOOD 1&2
CARTEL KILLAZ 1-3
DOPE GODS 1&2
By Hood Rich

THE STREETS ARE CALLING
By Duquie Wilson

STEADY MOBBN' 1-3
THE STREETS STAINED MY SOUL 1-3
By Marcellus Allen

WHO SHOT YA 1-3
SON OF A DOPE FIEND 1-4
HEAVEN GOT A GHETTO 1&2
SKI MASK MONEY 1&2
By Renta

GORILLAZ IN THE BAY 1-4
TEARS OF A GANGSTA 1/&2
3X KRAZY 1&2
STRAIGHT BEAST MODE 1&2
By DE'KARI

TRIGGADALE 1-3
MURDA WAS THE CASE 1-3
By Elijah R. Freeman

SLAUGHTER GANG 1-3
RUTHLESS HEART 1-3

By Willie Slaughter

GOD BLESS THE TRAPPERS 1-3
THESE SCANDALOUS STREETS 1-3
FEAR MY GANGSTA 1-5
THESE STREETS DON'T LOVE NOBODY 1-2
BURY ME A G 1-5
A GANGSTA'S EMPIRE 1-4
THE DOPEMAN'S BODYGAURD 1&2
THE REALEST KILLAZ 1-3
THE LAST OF THE OGS 1-3
By Tranay Adams

MARRIED TO A BOSS 1-3
By Destiny Skai & Chris Green

KINGZ OF THE GAME 1-7
CRIME BOSS 1-3
By Playa Ray

FUK SHYT
By Blakk Diamond

DON'T F#CK WITH MY HEART 1&2
By Linnea

ADDICTED TO THE DRAMA 1-3
IN THE ARM OF HIS BOSS
By Jamila

LOYALTY AIN'T PROMISED 1&2

By Keith Williams

YAYO 1-4
A SHOOTER'S AMBITION 1&2
BRED IN THE GAME
By S. Allen

TRAP GOD 1-3
RICH $AVAGE 1-3
MONEY IN THE GRAVE 1-3
CARTEL MONEY
By Martell Troublesome Bolden

FOREVER GANGSTA 1&2
GLOCKS ON SATIN SHEETS 1&2
By Adrian Dulan

TOE TAGZ 1-4
LEVELS TO THIS SHYT 1&2
IT'S JUST ME AND YOU
By Ah'Million

KINGPIN DREAMS 1-3
RAN OFF ON DA PLUG
By Paper Boi Rari

THE STREETS MADE ME 1-3
By Larry D. Wright

CONFESSIONS OF A GANGSTA 1-4
CONFESSIONS OF A JACKBOY 1-3

CONFESSIONS OF A HITMAN
By Nicholas Lock

I'M NOTHING WITHOUT HIS LOVE
SINS OF A THUG
TO THE THUG I LOVED BEFORE
A GANGSTA SAVED XMAS
IN A HUSTLER I TRUST
By Monet Dragun

QUIET MONEY 1-3
THUG LIFE 1-3
EXTENDED CLIP 1&2
A GANGSTA'S PARADISE
By Trai'Quan

CAUGHT UP IN THE LIFE 1-3
THE STREETS NEVER LET GO 1-3
By Robert Baptiste

NEW TO THE GAME 1-3
MONEY, MURDER & MEMORIES 1-3
By Malik D. Rice

CREAM 2-3
THE STREETS WILL TALK
By Yolanda Moore

THE STREETS WILL NEVER CLOSE 1-3
By K'ajji

LIFE OF A SAVAGE 1-4
A GANGSTA'S QUR'AN 1-4
MURDA SEASON 1-3
GANGLAND CARTEL 1-3
CHI'RAQ GANGSTAS 1-4
KILLERS ON ELM STREET 1-3
JACK BOYZ N DA BRONX 1-3
A DOPEBOY'S DREAM 1-3
JACK BOYS VS DOPE BOYS 1-3
COKE GIRLZ
COKE BOYS
SOSA GANG 1&2
BRONX SAVAGES
BODYMORE KINGPINS
BLOOD OF A GOON
By Romell Tukes

CONCRETE KILLA 1-3
VICIOUS LOYALTY 1-3
By Kingpen

THE ULTIMATE SACRIFICE 1-6
KHADIFI
IF YOU CROSS ME ONCE 1-3
ANGEL 1-4
IN THE BLINK OF AN EYE
By Anthony Fields

THE LIFE OF A HOOD STAR
By Ca$h & Rashia Wilson

NIGHTMARES OF A HUSTLA 1-3
BLOOD AND GAMES 1&2
By King Dream

GHOST MOB
By Stilloan Robinson

HARD AND RUTHLESS 1&2
MOB TOWN 251
THE BILLIONAIRE BENTLEYS 1-3
REAL G'S MOVE IN SILENCE
By Von Diesel

MOB TIES 1-7
SOUL OF A HUSTLER, HEART OF A KILLER 1-3
GORILLAZ IN THE TRENCHES
By SayNoMore

BODYMORE MURDERLAND 1-3
THE BIRTH OF A GANGSTER 1-4
By Delmont Player

FOR THE LOVE OF A BOSS 1&2
By C. D. Blue

KILLA KOUNTY 1-5
By Khufu

MOBBED UP 1-4
THE BRICK MAN 1-5
THE COCAINE PRINCESS 1-10

STEPPERS 1-3
SUPER GREMLIN 1-4
By King Rio

MONEY GAME 1&2
By Smoove Dolla

A GANGSTA'S KARMA 1-4
By FLAME

KING OF THE TRENCHES 1-3
By GHOST & TRANAY ADAMS

QUEEN OF THE ZOO 1&2
By Black Migo

GRIMEY WAYS 1-3
BETRAYAL OF A G
By Ray Vinci

XMAS WITH AN ATL SHOOTER
By Ca$h & Destiny Skai

KING KILLA 1&2
By Vincent "Vitto" Holloway

BETRAYAL OF A THUG 1&2
By Fre$h

THE MURDER QUEENS 1-5
By Michael Gallon

FOR THE LOVE OF BLOOD 1-4
By Jamel Mitchell

HOOD CONSIGLIERE 1&2
NO TIME FOR ERROR
By Keese

PROTÉGÉ OF A LEGEND 1&2
LOVE IN THE TRENCHES 1&2
By Corey Robinson

THE PLUG'S RUTHLESS DAUGHTER
By Tony Daniels

BORN IN THE GRAVE 1-3
CRIME PAYS
By Self Made Tay

MOAN IN MY MOUTH
By XTASY

TORN BETWEEN A GANGSTER AND A
GENTLEMAN
By J-BLUNT & Miss Kim

LOYALTY IS EVERYTHING 1-3
CITY OF SMOKE 1&2
By Molotti

HERE TODAY GONE TOMORROW 1&2
By Fly Rock

WOMEN LIE MEN LIE 1-4
FIFTY SHADES OF SNOW 1-3
STACK BEFORE YOU SPLURGE
GIRLS FALL LIKE DOMINOES
NAÏVE TO THE STREETS
By ROY MILLIGAN

PILLOW PRINCESS
By S. Hawkins

THE BUTTERFLY MAFIA 1-3
SALUTE MY SAVAGERY 1&2
By Fumiya Payne

THE LANE 1&2
By Ken-Ken Spence

THE PUSSY TRAP 1-5
By Nene Capri

DIRTY DNA
By Blaque

SANCTIFIED AND HORNY
by XTASY

BOOKS BY LDP'S CEO, CA$H

TRUST IN NO MAN

TRUST IN NO MAN 2

TRUST IN NO MAN 3

BONDED BY BLOOD

SHORTY GOT A THUG

THUGS CRY

THUGS CRY 2

THUGS CRY 3

TRUST NO BITCH

TRUST NO BITCH 2

TRUST NO BITCH 3

TIL MY CASKET DROPS

RESTRAINING ORDER

RESTRAINING ORDER 2

IN LOVE WITH A CONVICT

LIFE OF A HOOD STAR

XMAS WITH AN ATL SHOOTER

www.ingramcontent.com/pod-product-compliance
Lightning Source LLC
Chambersburg PA
CBHW070012120626
46591CB00026B/264